With a groan Carol said, "This is going to be a circus. We'll have PR people and lawyers falling over themselves to find out what's happened to their clients' records."

"Not to mention," said Bourke, laughing, "those frozen samples of high-society sperm and whatever." Abruptly, he sobered. "And frozen embryos. Destroying them — it's almost like murder, isn't it?"

LOOKING FOR NAIAD?

PAST DUE

THE 10TH DETECTIVE INSPECTOR CAROL ASHTON MYSTERY

CLAIRE McNAB

Claire McNab

PAST DUE

THE 10TH DETECTIVE INSPECTOR CAROL ASHTON MYSTERY

CLAIRE McNAB

THE NAIAD PRESS, INC.
1998

Printed in the United States of America on acid-free paper
First Edition

Editor: Lila Empson
Cover designer: Bonnie Liss (Phoenix Graphics)
Typesetter: Sandi Stancil

Library of Congress Cataloging-in-Publication Data

McNab, Claire.
    Past due / by Claire McNab.
        p. cm. — (A Detective Inspector Carol Ashton mystery : 10)
    ISBN 1-56280-217-8   (alk. paper)
    1. Ashton, Carol (Fictitious character)—Fiction. 2. Police-
women — Australia — Fiction. 3. Lesbians — Australia — Fiction
I. Title. II. Series: McNab, Claire. A Detective Inspector Carol
Ashton mystery : 10.
PS3563.C3877P3   1998
813'.54—dc21   98-13237
                                                              CIP

For Sheila

Acknowledgments

As always, my profound gratitude to Lila Empson and to Sandi Stancil, whose extraordinary editing and typesetting efforts have brought this book to actuality.

ABOUT THE AUTHOR

CLAIRE McNAB is the author of ten Detective Inspector Carol Ashton mysteries: *Lessons in Murder, Fatal Reunion, Death Down Under, Cop Out, Dead Certain, Body Guard, Double Bluff, Inner Circle, Chain Letter* and *Past Due*. She has written two romances, *Under the Southern Cross* and *Silent Heart,* and has co-authored a self-help book, *The Loving Lesbian,* with Sharon Gedan.

In her native Australia she is known for her crime fiction, plays, children's novels and self-help books.

Now permanently resident in Los Angeles, Claire teaches fiction writing in the UCLA Extension Writers' Program. She makes it a point to return to Australia once a year to refresh her Aussie accent.

PROLOGUE

Is this what it means to experience total dissociation? I was so furiously angry a few moments ago, so full of rage I lost it, absolutely lost it. It was exhilarating, satisfying, to let go of everything, to hit him that hard.

I heard his skull crack, and from that moment I was calm, outside myself. I remember watching the blood spray at each blow, hearing myself grunt with the effort, and noticing the dying sounds he made. And through all this I felt nothing but a detached interest.

So this is what it's like to kill someone.

Fear and disgust will come later, I'm sure of that, but now I'm irritated that splashing the petrol around is taking so much time. I've got to be careful not to get any on myself.

I could almost smile. How stupid it would be for me to go up in flames along with the clinic and his body.

CHAPTER ONE

"Amateur," said Hanover, the arson investigator, her scorn evident. "Splashed accelerant around this lab and the office next door, struck a match, and hoped for the best." She wrinkled her freckled nose. "Petrol. You can still smell it."

Stocky, her hair a frizz of auburn, she stood with hands on hips and surveyed the wreckage of the laboratory. Beside her, Carol stifled a yawn. She hadn't had her customary early morning jog or the several mugs of black coffee that usually jolted her into alertness. The call had come in before dawn, and

3

she'd dressed hastily in casual navy pants and top and flat shoes. Before she got into her car she'd whispered an apology to her neighbor's German shepherd, Olga, who'd been waiting hopefully at the fence for Carol to take her on a run through the bush.

Carol studied the laboratory. The sprinkler system hadn't been activated by the flames, so the damage was extensive. Carol could visualize the room as it had been. She'd seen the room, or one very like it, in some of the many self-promoting television appearances Dr. Brin Halstead had made during the last year.

Matching the elegant two-story, black-and-white exterior of the building, the laboratory walls and sleek benches had been pristine white. The rooms had held a variety of impressive laboratory instruments and gleaming machines. The glossy black floor, improbably, had seemed to be marble. And presiding over it, white coated, was the scientist-at-the-cutting-edge persona that Brin Halstead had cultivated. Carol remembered wondering if such photogenic perfection could really be a working lab or if it was something just for show, and was Halstead really a world-class fertility expert or was he an actor playing one?

The doctor would be pained to see the laboratory now. Water stood in pools or dripped from the seared ceiling, part of which had collapsed into the room. There was a greasy film over everything, and the heat had buckled the smooth white surfaces of the benches, burned away the upholstered seats of the black lab stools, exploded the computer monitor, and reduced instruments to lumps of melted glass and metal. Through the blackened, cracked glass of a wide picture window, the shrubs of an internal courtyard showed a blurred green. And everywhere the harsh stench of acrid smoke mingled with the unmistakable smell of scorched meat.

Hanover indicated the ceiling. "There's nothing wrong with the automatic sprinkler system. It would have worked well, had it come on, but someone turned the water off, which meant the hydraulically-operated alarm bell didn't function either. Sheer luck the cleaners came in when they did, or the whole building could have gone."

"Are you sure the accelerant was petrol?"

"Pretty sure, but I'll have a definite for you later today."

They were interrupted by Robinson, a novice crime-scene technician, whom Carol had only seen once before. "Inspector Ashton? They're moving the body now." He spoke in a ringing, self-confident tone, but his face had a greenish pallor.

Carol nodded. "Fine." She inclined her head toward the cluster of people gathered around the body in the middle of the lab. "Pretty rough?"

It seemed she'd ruffled his pride. "Seen worse," he said, a little too loud. He hesitated, as though wondering if he should add anything, then he gave an awkward nod and hurried away.

Hanover gave a sympathetic grunt. "Nasty," she said. "But I reckon the guy was dead before the fire. Even charred that way, you can see his head was smashed in." She flipped a page in her notebook and moved away to study the pattern of scorching on the ceiling tiles.

Carol hadn't looked closely at the body — she

5

would have to do that at the postmortem — but that first glance at the grotesque, blackened carcass, contorted by the extreme heat of the fire, would dance at the edge of her imagination for a long time.

"It's Robinson's first crispy critter," said an American voice behind Carol. "He'll be outside tossing his cookies, any moment now."

Hiding her dislike, Carol turned to Rafe Janach. "Crispy critter?" she said. "A charming Americanism." Her tone was pleasant, and she felt sure that he had no idea what she thought of him. It had nothing to do with the fact that he had replaced her friend Liz Carey as head of the crime-scene team. Her aversion was based on something much more basic — a gut instinct that told her he was trouble. He had impeccable credentials from the States, seemed easy to work with, and delivered reports with admirable speed, but Carol sensed a sneering, denigrating side to him that came out in the faint smirk he sometimes wore, or the put-downs she heard him use on others, particularly women.

"So what would you Aussies say?" Janach asked, grinning. "A toasted cobber?"

Detective Sergeant Mark Bourke, moving close to them to get out of the way of the stretcher bearing the remains, gave Janach a mock frown. "Don't even try to master our slang, mate. You'll have Buckley's chance of getting it right."

Carol smiled at Bourke. He was solid, dependable, and deceptively bland, and she valued his professionalism more than that of anyone else she had worked with in the police service. Carol didn't have many close friends, but Mark was one she trusted unconditionally.

Janach spread his hands. "Just trying to assimilate."

Carol couldn't help but compare the two men. Though they were of similar height, they couldn't have been more different in looks or demeanor. Rafe Janach was greyhound thin, and moved restlessly, constantly gesturing with his long hands. He had sharp features and thick, fair hair. One of the first things he'd said to Carol was, "Well, well, another blond. We *do* have more fun, don't we?"

Mark Bourke, increasingly self-conscious about his retreating hairline, had a very short crew cut, as if to minimize the contrast between scalp and his indeterminate brown hair. Physically he was strongly built, and he moved with a deliberate economy that was reflected in everything he did. His writing was neat, his desk immaculate, his case notes irreproachable.

Carol cleared her throat. The smell of the place was getting to her. She knew it would be in her clothes, in her hair. She said to Janach, "What've you got so far, Rafe?"

"Nothing that looks like a weapon, though we won't know what we're really looking for until after the postmortem. We have got a scorched jerry can that probably held gasoline." He made a wide gesture. "Take a look. There's a lot of stuff to sift through yet in the lab, and we haven't even started on the office or the rooms upstairs. It'll take the rest of the day, at least."

Carol gave Bourke an interrogative look and he responded, "No forced entry, Carol. The window cracked from the heat, not from an attempt to get in, not that anyone could have come that way, as it's a fully enclosed courtyard. The fire was discovered when the regular two-person cleaning team arrived around ten last night, and it hadn't been burning very long or the whole building would have been destroyed."

"And no one thought Halstead, or anyone else, would be inside?"

"Apparently Halstead preferred to come in very early in the day and expected his staff to do the same. That's why the cleaning was always done in the evening. The body wasn't found until three this morning when the fire brigade hazard team was mopping up. Anne's taking statements from the cleaners right now. Do you want to see them yourself?"

"Not at the moment. I'm sure she can handle it."

Anne Newsome had won Carol's trust over several cases, and Carol was confident that the young constable would cover all the necessary questions with her customary thoroughness.

Bourke said, "So the scenario is that Halstead lets someone in — there are strict security measures for the Clinic, so all doors are secured at all times — and whoever it is smashes Halstead's head to pulp, pours petrol everywhere, lights it, and gets out of here."

"Having the petrol handy suggests premeditation," said Carol.

"I don't know," said Janach, who'd been listening with his narrow head cocked. "Some people carry gas in the trunk as a precaution against running dry, don't they?"

"Pretty cool," said Bourke, "to impulsively batter someone to death and then have the presence of mind to go outside to your car to collect something to start a fire."

Janach shrugged. "I could do it."

Carol, impatient with Janach's presence, said, "It would help if we had a weapon. That would give some idea of whether the murder was premeditated or not."

Her pointed tone wasn't lost on Janach. "I better get back to it, then," he said with a thin smile.

Watching Janach's retreating back, Bourke said, "You don't like him much, do you?"

"I'm indifferent, just so long as he does his job."

Bourke looked at her sideways. "Yeah?" It was clear he didn't entirely believe her. "I get the feeling he doesn't altogether appreciate women in positions of authority."

"Too bad," said Carol, dismissing the subject. "Now, the corpse — are you sure it's Halstead?"

"There's no way we'll get a visual identification, but I'd say it's him. Underneath the body when they moved it a few minutes ago they found the keys to a Beemer — and a BMW registered to him is parked in the loading dock — plus a wallet with license and credit cards in his name."

"Handy they weren't incinerated."

"Dental records should show for sure if it's him." He raised an eyebrow. "You're thinking Halstead would fake his own death?"

Carol thought of the scandal that had recently engulfed Halstead Clinic, to the delight of the media, who had reported with gusto the details of the court case where a former client was suing Brin Halstead over fertility treatment, claiming that the baby his

9

wife delivered wasn't genetically related to either parent. The draconian Australian defamation laws made it difficult, but the media had managed to hint at further cases with even more sensational details. There had been much disappointment when the matter was abruptly settled out of court for an undisclosed sum.

"I know it's far-fetched," said Carol, "but I have the feeling a Houdini act is something Brin Halstead might do."

"His partner, Dr. Vail, might throw some light on that," said Bourke. "He's waiting outside, and not very patiently. Seems he's got security worries about the confidential material in the clinic. He kept on mentioning high-profile clients, as though that would be a magic password in to see you."

With a groan Carol said, "This is going to be a circus. We'll have PR people and lawyers falling over themselves to find out what's happened to their clients' records."

"Not to mention," said Bourke, laughing, "those frozen samples of high-society sperm and whatever." Abruptly, he sobered. "And frozen embryos. Destroying them — it's almost like murder, isn't it?"

CHAPTER TWO

The basement had utilitarian concrete floors and walls, in contrast to the careful appearance of the floors above. A generator hummed in one corner, near a series of chrome tubs and industrial refrigerator units.

Carol was examining the shutoff valve for the sprinkler system while a technician fingerprinted the area when a sudden thought struck her. She glanced at her watch. "Hell!"

Grabbing her cellular phone, she punched in the

number and moved impatiently around while the phone rang. "Eleanor? It's Carol. David hasn't left yet, has he?"

While her ex-husband's wife went to look for David, Carol thought of how much she loved her son and how relatively little she saw of him, especially now that he'd reached his teens and had, it seemed, countless things competing for his attention. She was uneasily aware of how often she made stern resolutions to set aside time for him and how frequently the demands of her job got in the way.

"Hello?" Even with that one word David sounded cautious, cool.

"Darling, I'm sorry. I know I said I'd be at your school sports day, but —"

"Mum, you promised!"

"I know I did, and I meant it, but something urgent's come up. I might get away for an hour or so."

"You won't, Mum." His disgust was obvious.

"David, you know how much I wanted to be there to see you run."

"Yeah, sure."

"But I'll still pick you up on Saturday."

"Mum, I've got things to do this weekend, okay, so don't bother."

Keenly aware that he was punishing her for yet again breaking a pledge to make time for him in her life, Carol said, "David, I do want to see you."

"Gotta go, Mum, or I'll be late. Bye."

Snapping the phone shut, she made a mental note to call him this afternoon. Or perhaps she *could* steal a few hours and at least make an appearance at the school. She shrugged that thought away. At this stage in an investigation, it was impossible.

She ran up the metal fire escape two stairs at a time, thinking ruefully that this would probably be her exercise for the day. The fire door opened into the corridor outside the laboratory. Bourke was approaching with a slight man who seemed so anxious to get to her that he was elbowing Bourke out of the way. He had thin dark hair and emphatically arched eyebrows that gave him a look of constant surprise.

"Dr. William Vail —" Bourke began. He wasn't allowed to finish.

"Inspector Ashton? I've been waiting for some considerable time, and I have two staff members outside who must be given permission to enter the building."

"What are their names?"

"Gilda Milton is Dr. Halstead's personal assistant. She's been standing in the street using my cell phone to contact staff members to tell them not to come to work. Several times a police officer told her to move on and I had to intervene."

His glare made it clear he was inclined to hold Carol personally responsible for this. "And aside from Gilda, I must have Tom Lorant. He's in charge of the technical side of the clinic, and I'll be needing him with me to help assess the damage."

He rushed on, "I don't know if you're aware, but some very important patients are served by the Halstead Clinic. Very important. It's unconscionable that any Tom, Dick, and Harry can be tramping around the premises while I'm refused entry!"

He was short, and lightly built, but his booming voice belonged to a much larger man. Carol could almost see his heels rising as he strained to attain her height and look her directly in the eye.

Noting that he hadn't even mentioned the death of his partner, Carol said mildly, "This is a secured area. I can assure you that only authorized personnel have entered it."

Dr. Vail's circumflex eyebrows shot up. "Your police people — I can understand that — but what about the firefighters in the middle of the night? Did anyone check their credentials?" He looked around the devastated laboratory. "Anything could have been taken . . ."

"There's an adjoining office that's also been extensively damaged," said Carol.

"The records!" Vail skirted a pile of collapsed roof tiles and hurried toward a doorway in the back wall of the lab. He pushed at the door, which had obviously once been shiny metal but was now blighted with patterns of dark colors from the heat of the flames. "This door should be locked. It's always kept locked."

He peered into the darkened room. "There's no light." He glared at Carol. "How can I see if there's no light?"

The pungent smell that gusted out at them stung the back of Carol's throat. Beside her, Bourke produced a flashlight and played its beam into the room. Metal file drawers had been pulled out, and the shells of two monitors gaped open, their screens destroyed. The floor was covered with the remains of burned paper and melted plastic.

"My God." Vail was obviously stunned. "Who could have done this?"

Carol said, "I'll arrange for Ms. Milton to join you, and one of my officers will accompany you while you do a room-by-room inventory of the entire clinic. If anything's missing, we need to know about it as soon as possible. Perhaps you can start in the undamaged section of the building. After scene-of-crime has finished here, you can see if anything's salvageable in this office. Lights will be set up by then."

Carol found herself watching with fascination as his extraordinary eyebrows descended in a frown. "That will have to wait. First I have to check the basement. If the emergency generator didn't kick in for the freezing units, it'll be a disaster. A disaster!"

"As a matter of urgency I also require a comprehensive list of all patients and all staff."

Her question made him bounce with indignation. "That's impossible. Quite impossible. There are privacy issues. I can't give you names without permission from the people concerned."

Bourke said, "I'm afraid privacy takes a backseat in a suspicious death investigation."

"Suspicious death?" Vail looked from one to the other. "Are you saying Brin was deliberately killed?"

He seemed so surprised that Carol asked, "What was your first thought when you heard his body had been found?"

Vail moved his shoulders uncomfortably. "I don't know . . ." He brushed a hand over his lank hair.

"Well, if you must know, I thought Brin was hoist with his own petard. You know, he set the place on fire and got caught in it."

"That's interesting," said Bourke, taking out his notebook and pen. "Exactly why would you think that?"

"You know . . ." Vail made a vague gesture, eyeing the notebook with suspicion. "You must have heard. The clinic was in trouble."

"The court case? The bad publicity?"

Vail scowled at Bourke's blunt questions. "Yes, that, of course, but Brin was in financial trouble, too. I don't know the details" — he gave a sour smile — "as Brin didn't believe in sharing information, even if it might have a vital effect on me."

"Could you be more specific?" said Carol.

Her tone was pleasant, but Vail's was face closed. "I don't believe I can."

"When did you last see Dr. Halstead?"

He looked at her with suspicion. "I didn't see him last night, if that's what you mean."

"When did you see him?"

"I didn't pay much attention. Why would I, having no idea *this* was going to happen?" He sounded aggrieved. "The best I can estimate — and this may not be totally accurate — is six-fifteen, when I was packing up for the day. Met Brin in the washroom, actually."

"Did he say anything about his plans for the evening?"

"Of course not. I mean, we were colleagues, but our personal lives were just that — personal."

"And after you left work? Did you go home?"

"I don't see what business it is of yours —" He

broke off, then said grudgingly, "Yes I went straight home. Spent the evening with my wife. I hope that satisfies you." He looked at Bourke, seeming to only then realize that he was taking notes. "Perhaps I should have legal representation," he said. "I don't want to say too much. I know how you cops twist things."

"These are just routine questions," said Carol. She didn't look in Bourke's direction, as it was likely he was hiding a smile at her use of the standard misstatement, so beloved of fictional detectives. There were no routine questions in a homicide case.

When she'd arrived at the clinic it had barely been dawn, so Carol decided to go outside and reconnoiter in daylight. As soon as she entered the lobby area, she could see through the chrome-edged entrance doors a flurry of activity in the media contingent outside. Ignoring the cameras turned her way, she examined the lobby. The smell of smoke pervaded the area, but there was no visible damage. Light poured through a glass roof, two stories above. At intervals down the shiny black walls were alcoves where the luxuriant fronds of ferns spilled over in green cascades. Carol fleetingly wondered how they were tended. Whatever system was used, they were annoyingly greener and thicker than the ferns she cultivated at home.

The back wall of the entrance area was broken by a wide opening flanked by two huge blue ceramic pots containing more greenery. Through the opening was a reception area furnished with deep chairs in black leather. In contrast, the entrance to the corridor that led to the laboratories was an insignificant door with only the word *Private* inscribed.

The floor of the entrance area was glossy white, but its perfection had been smeared and scuffed by the traffic to and from the ruins of the laboratory. Behind the gleaming reception module — Carol decided *desk* was too pedestrian a term — THE HALSTEAD CLINIC appeared in discreet blue lettering. There were no security cameras. Carol wondered with a wry smile if this omission might be on account of the reticence of celebrity clients, who might not welcome any recording of their visit to a fertility clinic, however upscale it might be.

The double doors opened soundlessly as she approached them. In early summer it was still cool in the mornings, but the brassy glare promised a hot afternoon. Carol said a few words to the uniformed officer guarding the building before going out into the street to survey the area. The Halstead Clinic was on a side street in Paddington, just off the eternal bustle of Oxford Street. Carol had ordered the immediate area closed, and traffic barriers barred each end of the short block.

"Carol!"

"Inspector Ashton!"

The media had appropriated part of the closure and chafed behind crime-scene tape, along with various members of the public who had gathered in the hope that something interesting would happen. At Carol's appearance, reporters and videographers were galvanized into action to record something — anything — for the evening news.

Carol acknowledged them with a brief inclination of her head, then turned her attention to the building and its immediate environs. The clinic took up much of the block, and a great deal of money had been spent to create a dazzling edifice that spoke of refined luxury, not vulgar excess. THE HALSTEAD CLINIC again appeared in unembellished blue letters by the side of the shallow black steps that led to the entrance doors. Gleaming white walls had their chaste surface inset at intervals with black geometric designs. Smoke-gray tinted windows were edged with sparkling chrome.

A third of the block was taken up by the parking area. It was difficult to make a parking lot elegant, but this one had ebony pillars at its entrance and was artfully landscaped to give the impression that one was parking in a tailored grove of shrubbery and trees. Carol walked around it, considering how easy it would be to find cover and escape detection.

A lane ran at the rear of the building. Here the white wall was unadorned and the loading dock a functional gray. The heavy mesh electric door was down and locked, but by pressing her face close to it Carol was able to see the outlines of Halstead's BMW inside.

She continued around the building, finding a fire door on the other side. It could only be opened from the inside, and had, she knew, a spring mechanism that snapped it shut immediately after the door was released. None of the windows was designed to be opened, and there was no sign that any window near ground level had been tampered with. It was clear that there were only three possible entry points to the building, and it was most likely that the front entrance or the loading dock had provided the murderer a way in.

Her reappearance on the other side of the clinic encouraged one bold TV reporter to duck under the tape and approach her. Shoving a microphone in Carol's direction, the toothy young man said in breathless tones, "A reliable source says that Dr. Halstead was stabbed to death before the fire. Can you confirm that, Inspector?"

Carol had a moment's amusement at this guess. Very little official information had been released, other than the fact that a body, believed to be that of Dr. Brin Halstead, had been found in a burned lab at his clinic. It was a classic news-gathering trick to invent a detail and try to get a response that would give some indication of the true facts. She could make his day by saying, "Stabbed? No, we think Dr. Halstead was bludgeoned to death."

Instead she said smoothly, "I've no comment at this time."

Ignoring him, she turned to survey the buildings across the road from the clinic. At the end farthest from Oxford Street was a private home with a high brick wall blankly facing the street. Directly opposite was another office building, single-story and an anonymous beige. Carol could see a notice board with a list of tenants by the door. She could also see several people behind the windows gazing out at the activity outside.

Making a mental note to send someone to interview everyone in both buildings, she took a deep breath untainted by anything but vehicle exhaust fumes and prepared to go back to the cloying, smoke-scented air of the clinic.

"Excuse me." The voice was high-pitched and breathy.

Carol looked around to see a woman wearing black pants and an oversize top that swamped her fragile body. She had a long face and thin, nervous hands. Her dark hair, lightly streaked with gray, fell past her narrow shoulders.

The uniformed officer beside the woman said, "I'm sorry, Inspector, but this lady insisted that she had something important to tell you."

"I'm Ursula Vail," she said, showing small white teeth in a fleeting smile. She didn't look directly at Carol but kept her head slightly bent as she gazed somewhere past her shoulder. "I drove my husband here. He's inside."

"It's okay," Carol said to the officer, who moved back to his post.

"I wanted to have a private word with you."

There was an underlying whine in Ursula Vail's voice that Carol had already decided was likely to go from irritating to downright exasperating in short order.

Carol said, "How can I help you?"

"I think it's rather that *I* can help you." Ursula Vail stepped closer, her eyes averted. Carol caught the scent of a heavy musk perfume.

"You see, Inspector," Ursula Vail went on, "my husband is honorable and loyal, so he'll think it his duty to conceal all the things that Brin Halstead has done. *I* don't have any such scruples."

"Perhaps we can speak later." Carol didn't want

to alienate a possible source of information, but any interviews with Vail's wife would be in the future when the investigation had progressed beyond the initial stages.

"Of course, you're right," said Ursula Vail. "You won't want to be bothered now. Just tell Bill that he's to call me on the mobile phone when he wants me to pick him up. Would you do that, please?"

"Ms. Vail?" said Carol as the woman turned to go. "Just routine, but would you mind telling me how you spent last evening?"

Ursula Vail seemed pleased to be asked the question. "Why, I was with Bill, at home. I got in about six, and he arrived at his usual time, around seven-thirty. We had dinner, and then the two of us spent the rest of the evening in a slothful way in front of the television. Not that I watch it closely. I do prefer to read or knit. Do something useful. Anyway, I believe we went to bed early, around ten-thirty, only to be woken with the dreadful news about the clinic."

Carol thanked her, then watched as she hurried across the street. Ursula Vail's answer had sounded rehearsed. It had been Carol's experience that a person who was lying often gave too much information in an effort to convince. But then, Carol had to admit, it was a question so obvious, in the circumstances, that almost anyone would have thought of how they'd respond.

Carol sent someone down to the basement to give Vail the message from his wife, then found Rafe Janach for a progress report. They were conferring when Bourke came up from the basement followed by Vail and a thick-waisted, motherly woman who Carol assumed was Gilda Milton, Brin Halstead's personal assistant. She didn't have to guess the name of the man behind her. He wore a name tag on his white coat: THOMAS LORANT.

The doctor was bursting with indignation. "The liquid nitrogen containers — they look okay, but someone's tampered with them." He turned to the two behind him. "That's right, isn't it, Tom? Gilda?"

"Seems so," said Tom Lorant. He was robustly built, and taller than Bourke. The contrast between the two men and the doctor made Vail seem even smaller than he actually was.

Lorant gave Carol a slight smile, almost lost under his dark mustache. "There's quite some cleaning up to do," he said. He had a soft, agreeable voice. It was as though, with his size, he never needed to raise it to be noticed.

Dr. Vail had his eyes fixed on the woman. "Gilda, you agree? There's been tampering?"

It interested Carol to see that Dr. Vail needed validation for his opinion, even from someone who presumably knew nothing about the technical side of the organization.

"I'm sure you're right, Dr. Vail," Gilda Milton said. She had the manner of one who could soothe fractious children, or adults.

"Anyone could have opened the containers, and caused irreparable damage," growled Vail. He looked pointedly at Carol. "One of your people, just snooping around, for example."

"We will need fingerprints from the three of you," said Carol. When Vail bristled, she added with a slight smile, "Only for elimination purposes. Everyone who has any access to the clinic has to be finger-printed so that any foreign prints can be isolated."

"Dr. Vail seems to think that some samples have been removed," said Bourke.

"*Seems* to think? I *know* frozen embryos, not to mention other tissue samples, have been interfered with, and I believe some have been taken. Tom will support me on that."

"More and more interesting," said Janach. "What use would any of these embryos be to anyone?"

Vail shot him a look of dislike. "The Halstead Clinic is at the forefront of genetic engineering. I imagine any of our competitors would be more than interested in our research."

Janach was unimpressed. "But without ancillary information — lab notes detailing the experiments, logs, reports, etcetera — nothing that was taken would be of any use to a competitor, would it, Dr. Vail?"

"I don't imagine you're in a position to judge," snapped Vail.

"An inventory of the laboratory records will show if anything's been taken," said Gilda Milton.

Carol, not wanting the doctor to become even more uncooperative than he was already threatening to be, gave Janach a warning glance, then said to Vail, "It's very helpful to have guidance about the operation of the clinic, and we appreciate how difficult this is for you."

Somewhat mollified, Vail allowed himself to be led away by Bourke. Lorant meekly followed, and Gilda Milton, after giving Carol an amused look, went after the men.

Janach, watching them go, said to Carol, "We only

have Vail's word on what's going on here, and it's way out of my area of expertise. We just might have to bring in an expert to evaluate the situation."

Carol nodded. It was obvious she'd have to do a crash course in fertility and genetic issues to have the necessary background that this case was going to demand. "Maybe," she said to Janach, "it's really simple, and we're trying to make it complicated. Just a common burglary, gone wrong."

Janach's sharp-featured face broke into a grin. "Dream on, Carol," he said.

CHAPTER THREE

The phone on Carol's desk rang for what seemed the hundredth time. The death of a celebrity doctor like Halstead had brought an avalanche of attention to the chief investigating officer, and Carol, used as she was to media attention, felt tired and irritable. She moved an empty coffee mug, shoved a bundle of files out of the way, and snatched up the receiver.

"Carol Ashton."

"It's Madeline, Carol."

"Yes?" Carol was momentarily amused to hear the

caution in her tone. She could see Madeline as vividly as if she had been sitting across the desk from her — exquisitely dressed, her copper hair smoothly sweeping to her shoulders, her wide gray eyes deceptively innocent.

"Don't worry, darling." Madeline's husky voice had a confiding timbre. "This isn't personal. I hear Brin Halstead has been burned to a positive crisp."

Carol sighed to herself. Madeline was indefatigable when it came to getting an exclusive for her television show, *The Shipley Report*. "Madeline, why don't you go through the usual channels? There's nothing much I can tell you."

"The usual channels?" Madeline snorted. "You mean the hacks in police PR? My researchers can deal with them."

"And you can deal with me?"

Madeline gave a silky laugh. "You said it, darling, although you haven't given me the chance for quite some time."

"I've got no comment about Halstead's death."

"It's murder, isn't it?"

Carol repressed a sigh. "Homicide hasn't been confirmed."

"Not a homicide? He bashed his own head in, concealed the murder weapon, turned off the fire sprinklers, then doused himself in petrol and struck a match?"

It didn't surprise Carol that Madeline was well abreast of the available information. She used any means — sheer hard work, charm, intimidation, barter — to get what she wanted. And as her image every weeknight went out to a large proportion of television sets in use, Madeline could rely on her own celebrity status to inveigle reluctant interviewees in front of her cameras.

Curious, Carol said, "Still no comment, but who told you those details?"

"I always protect my sources," said Madeline with mock offense. "You, of all people, should know that."

It was true. Ruthless though she was in pursuit of a story, Madeline always played by the unwritten rules, so she was trusted by a wide variety of anonymous people, many in high positions of business or government, who would leak her information before her media competitors even knew that there *was* a story.

"I can't give you any more than the official line."

"Oh, come *on,* Carol. Just some little exclusive. Anything. What if I give you something in return?"

Carol found herself smiling. This was the Madeline Shipley she knew so well. "What is this something?"

"Let's put it this way — this is a much bigger story than you could imagine."

"Tantalizing, but vague."

"I'll give you a snippet of information, but you better reciprocate big-time, because what I'm about to tell you will knock your socks off."

Carol chuckled. "Make it good. I'm finding it hard to think of what would live up to this prepublicity."

"Okay. No names, but there's a whistle-blower in the Halstead Clinic who's got proof that the good doctor was offering cloning services to those who were willing to pay. And more — none are born yet, but there are some cloned babies near term."

"Cloning? What is this, Madeline? Science fiction? I think someone's putting you on."

For once, she'd been able to offend Madeline. "No one puts me on, darling," she snapped. "I check everything out — and this is true blue."

"The name of the whistle-blower?"

"You know I can't tell you, but you only need to know there is one. Eventually you'll find out who." Her tone became warmer as she continued. "Carol, I've given you something valuable. What are you going to give me?"

"I can't give you an exclusive, but I promise you'll be first with any information being released."

Madeline clicked her tongue in annoyance. "That's the best you ever offer me."

"Take it or leave it."

"How soon before the others?"

Carol rolled her eyes to the ceiling. "As early as possible. That'll have to do."

"You'll call me yourself?"

"If you're lucky."

"Excellent," said Madeline. "You know how I love to hear your voice."

As Carol put down the receiver, Anne Newsome came into her office, radiating her usual olive-skinned good health and enthusiasm. "The cleaners' statements," she said, putting typed pages on top of the pile in front of Carol.

Gesturing Anne to a seat, Carol said, "Give me a summary."

"Long-term cleaners, both of them. Sid Mann's been doing the Halstead Clinic, as well as both Halstead's and Dr. Vail's homes, for six years. The younger one, Dot Rayner, has been with the cleaning firm for five years. No criminal records, not even a speeding ticket between them."

"I imagine they haven't remembered anything useful, or you would have been here earlier."

Anne grinned at Carol's dry tone. "You're so right. They arrived together in a small truck at ten sharp. Dot says she's sure because the radio station they had on gave the time just as they got there. Nothing odd about the parking area. Except for their vehicle, it was empty. And there were no furtive figures running off into the darkness to alert them that something was wrong."

"Have you seen the parking area? There's plenty of cover if someone wanted to hide."

"And they weren't looking for an intruder," said Anne, "so it doesn't mean much that they didn't notice anyone."

"Obviously the cleaners have keys to the clinic."

Anne nodded. "I'm making a list of everyone who has access. The clinic uses an electronic keycard system, where you slide a plastic card into a slot to open the front doors. There's a delivery bay at the back of the building, but to open that you have to have a separate keycard."

"I swear this was tidy yesterday." Carol shuffled papers on her desk. "I've got a floor plan of the building somewhere here. It was filed with the fire department." She found it and spread it out.

The Halstead Clinic was planned around a central enclosed courtyard. The ground floor was made up of a lobby that led into a reception and waiting area that looked out to the manicured shrubbery of the courtyard. To one side were two laboratories and several offices. The delivery dock at the back gave direct access to the labs and offices. The upper floor held smaller waiting rooms, two operating rooms with associated facilities, and staff rooms. Below ground level, the basement held a generator, refrigeration facilities, and storage areas.

Carol located her gold fountain pen and used it as a pointer. "So the cleaners parked by the side of the building, here?"

Anne bent her dark head over the diagram. "That's right. Then, when they were collecting their stuff from the truck, they noticed the smell of smoke, and as soon as they got around the front, they could see it billowing into the reception area. Sid told Dot to call for help, and he went into the building and grabbed a fire extinguisher, but there was nothing much he could do."

"So everything with the cleaners checks out?"

"Everything. Dot's call was logged at six minutes past ten, and the first fire engine arrived at ten-eighteen."

"And Sid didn't see anyone?"

Anne gave her a mischievous look. "If you're asking if a someone obligingly burst out of the lab and ran past him, waving a blunt instrument covered in blood, I'll have to disappoint you."

Carol frowned at the orderly surface of Bourke's desk. It was aggravating how tidy it was, with everything carefully aligned and an almost empty in-tray.

Bourke put down the phone, saying, "We've got an appointment with Halstead's wife at four-thirty this afternoon. That okay with you?"

"That's great. I want to have time to shower and change. All I can smell is smoke."

"I didn't talk to his wife, but to her mother, Iniga Alaric. We might kill two birds with one stone, as she announced she had no intention of leaving her daughter alone for us, as she put it, to upset her in this tragic time."

"Oh, great." Carol grimaced. Iniga and her developer husband, Perry Alaric, were formidable doyens of society and were seen at all the stellar events. The glossily elegant Iniga Alaric was likely to provide some difficulties. Carol had run into her once before at a function Bourke's wife had persuaded Carol to attend. Carol had not been impressed by Iniga Alaric's insincere electric smile and her dismissive 'Oh, you're that police officer who's on the news all the time" when they had been introduced.

Bourke broke into her thoughts. ". . . and I've got Maureen chasing up financial details. She can bluff information out of almost any institution, so we should know if Vail's right about Halstead being in money trouble."

Carol knew what he meant. Maureen Oatland was large in body, voice, and character, and could bulldoze her way through most obstacles. She didn't use finesse in her job as a detective, but her blunt style often got surprising results.

"What about the people in the buildings opposite the clinic?"

"No help. No one was in the office building across the road after six o'clock. There's a slew of little businesses there, but they all seem to shut up shop early. The cleaning's done first thing in the morning, so no joy there. As far as the private house on the corner is concerned, two old dears live there, deaf as posts. By nine they're tucked in and sound asleep."

"It was a warm night, so people would have been out walking, maybe going up to the shops on Oxford Street."

He gave a moan of protest. "It's going to be hard pulling people off other things to do a door-to-door of the whole district."

"Just the surrounding streets."

"Okay." He sounded resigned.

She could remember when she had been a young cop and had done her share of those frustrating, usually fruitless tasks. The experience of door knocking had given her a new respect for the members of those religions who sent their adherents proselytizing from door to door.

Perhaps it would be a waste of time, but so much of police work was numbing repetition of asking the same questions over and over until, if luck was smiling, you hit the jackpot.

"Halstead's post is tomorrow," said Bourke. "I got Jeff Duke to promise he'd bump other cases so he could fit it in. It's eleven tomorrow morning."

He grinned at Carol's expression. Postmortems were bad enough, but a burned body, like a floater — someone long drowned — could be particularly grim.

Carol, as she always did, shoved the thought of the macabre sights the morgue would offer to the back of her mind. "Mark," she said, "you know everything. I need the name of a geneticist who can explain cloning."

Bourke didn't even blink. "Pat *said* there was a rumor about cloning going around. I didn't believe it, of course. Where did you hear it?"

"Madeline Shipley. This rumor — did it mention Halstead?"

"Absolutely. I remember Pat telling me it was the talk of the last launch party at the gallery. Pat didn't believe it either — thought it was a hoot. And, after all, there's a law against cloning, so why would Halstead run the risk?"

In all the hysteria about the cloning of a Scottish lamb, Australia had been one of the many nations that had passed laws against human experiments in the area, but it had never occurred to Carol that this legislation would be anything but symbolic or that she would ever investigate the possibility that someone had carried out the procedure using human cells.

Bourke tapped his pen against his teeth. "Pat knows Joan Yaller at Sydney University pretty well. She's the expert everyone goes to when they want to explain to the public something complicated in the genetic area."

"Professor Yaller will do very well, and an introduction from Pat would be a help."

Pat James, tall, plain, and effervescently friendly, was Mark Bourke's wife of around three years. She had become Carol's friend. Although Pat's irreverent frankness didn't seem to fit into the world of the Art Gallery of New South Wales, she had been outstandingly successful in her position there and counted as friends or acquaintances many of the most influential members of Sydney society.

"Mark, this could just be empty gossip, although

Madeline says there's someone at the Halstead Clinic who was ready to blow the whistle about cloning. She wouldn't give me a name."

"If La Shipley says it's so, it is," said Bourke, grinning. "When I get a clinic staff list I'll have a look to see who'd be in a position to know what's going on." He shook his head. "Cloning, eh? It'll be time travel next."

CHAPTER FOUR

The Halsteads' residence was on the top floor of a luxurious block of apartments overlooking Sydney Harbour. After the heat outside, the cool, air-conditioned atmosphere of the lobby was a pleasant shock against Carol's bare arms. She had snatched the luxury of an hour to rush home, have a quick shower, wash her hair, and change into a pale green summer suit. Even so, she imagined she could still detect a faint suggestion of the smell of smoke.

Bourke identified them to the building attendant,

who was installed behind a paneled reception desk raised on a platform so that he looked down on lesser mortals. Everything in the entry radiated tasteful affluence, from the floor tiled in cream and burgundy to the understated abstract tapestry taking up one wall.

The small, burgundy-carpeted lift had rich wooden panels alternating with narrow, beveled mirrors. Catching sight of her multiple images, Carol was amused to find herself automatically checking her nose. The swelling was, she decided, finally subsiding. The plastic surgeon who had repaired the damage caused by the rifle butt that had smashed her nose had said it might take months to return to normal, but Carol still wasn't used to this not-so-subtle alteration to her appearance.

Bourke grinned at her. "You're still beautiful, Carol."

She laughed, embarrassed to be caught. "I was just contemplating whether to file a malpractice suit against the plastic surgeon," she said lightly.

As they stepped out of the lift on the penthouse floor, they were greeted by a carved wooden table with antique yellow china urns filled with arrangements of fresh flowers. Bourke said mockingly, "If I had to, I could force myself to live in a place like this."

Carol shook her head. "I couldn't. I have to have growing things around me — trees and birds and flowers."

Bourke had often admired Carol's Seaforth home, nestled in bushland above the gorgeous sweep of Middle Harbour. One day, at a barbecue in her garden, he'd said seriously, "If you ever think of selling, please give me first refusal. Pat agrees with me; we'd buy it in an instant."

She'd said without hesitation, "Sorry, it's not on the market."

Now she wondered if it was still true. Maybe, in the future, she might have to move. She gave a mental shrug. She'd worry about that some other time.

Contrary to Bourke's expectations, Iniga Alaric was not at the penthouse to protect her daughter. They were met at the door by her husband, Perry Alaric. He greeted them in an offhand way, as though, Carol thought, she and Bourke were quite unimportant in his scheme of things. "You've come to see my daughter. She's resting. I'll get her."

Carol had seen his sleepy-eyed face featured in the business pages countless times. He was a big man, but soft with fat, and the expensive suit he wore could not disguise his paunch. Although his expression was mild and he looked almost stupid, she knew him to be an outstandingly successful business-man who had grown the family company, Alaric Developments, into a multimillion-dollar firm that specialized in huge shopping centers and industrial parks.

He waved vaguely toward white leather chairs and a divan sitting in a semicircle in a sea of plush blue carpet. "I suppose you'd better sit," he said without enthusiasm. "I won't be a moment."

He was, however, considerably longer than a moment. Convinced that it was a technique to unsettle them, Carol leaned back in the elegant caress of the chair and contemplated the furnishings

— sleek and expensive — and then the world outside the plate glass wall. The beauties of Sydney Harbour were familiar, but she never tired of them.

The view from the penthouse was glorious. Carol could see the pale, soaring roofs of the Sydney Opera House contrasting against the dour gray arch of Sydney Harbour Bridge. Ferries, launches, and ships seemed to float on foil as the afternoon sun glittered on the expanse of water.

Glancing at Bourke, who was checking his notes, Carol thought of how good a team they made. An unspoken understanding, forged in countless hours of interviews, allowed them to work seamlessly together. Each of them sensed when to ask a question and when to be silent, and each had a sense of the pattern of actions and reactions that differed, however subtly, in every situation.

Carol smiled to herself. It was almost like a comfortable marriage, where each partner could read in the other the slightest change of expression, the nuances of tone that anyone else would miss.

Fifteen minutes passed, then twenty. Bourke raised his eyebrows to Carol, but didn't speak. Finally there was a whisper of noise and a woman wearing jeans and a pink, long-sleeve shirt came into the room alone.

"I'm Leta Halstead," she said in a clear, carrying voice.

Carol and Bourke rose, Carol introducing herself and Bourke and adding, "We're so sorry to intrude at this time."

She nodded, then sank down on the white divan. She was younger than Carol had expected. Gangly and awkward, she had a small, neat head on a long neck. Her cap of dark hair was short and brushed forward so it curled around her ears. Carol thought that if she were grief stricken over her husband's death, she concealed it admirably.

"Was Brin murdered?" Leta asked.

"It seems so," said Carol, matching her conversational tone.

Leta leaned forward to take a cigarette from an ebony box on the coffee table. She tapped the end against her thumbnail, then lit it with the heavy jet lighter. "Seems so? But surely you'd know, Inspector."

Watching her blow a stream of smoke, Carol said, "We'll have more information about your husband's death tomorrow."

The fact that Carol had avoided mentioning the postmortem seemed to touch Leta Halstead with fleeting amusement. The corners of her tight little mouth curved as she said, "You can be brutal, Inspector. I can take it." Her cheeks hollowed as she sucked on the cigarette. "Was Brin burned alive? I should think that would be a horrible way to go."

Such self-possession was almost unnerving. Carol wondered if she were drugged, although she wasn't slurring her words and the pupils of her eyes appeared quite normal.

Carol said, "At this point we don't have detailed information."

"Did you know your husband was going to the clinic last night?" Bourke asked.

Leta switched her gaze to him. "I had no idea. We had an early dinner, something light, and then he went out."

"What time did you eat?"

She made a graceful, vague gesture. "I don't

know. I didn't have anything, as I wasn't hungry. Brin made himself spaghetti and meat sauce."

"The time?"

His insistence, Carol knew, was to help ascertain time of death. The fire had made the use of body temperature indicators unreliable, so the much less accurate analysis of the stage of stomach contents would have to be utilized by the pathologist.

Leta gave the slightest of shrugs. "Around seven-thirty, eight, I suppose. Brin said, I think, that he had some meeting with colleagues at one of the big hotels. But then, I didn't pay much attention."

"Would there be a note in his appointment book, something like that? We do need to trace his movements yesterday."

She considered Bourke's words. "Well, Sergeant — it is Sergeant, isn't it? The fact is that you couldn't rely on Brin to tell the truth. He could have been doing anything, going anywhere. I've tried to find him too many times, only to discover he wasn't there."

Turning her head to look at Carol, she went on, "I come from a family of liars, Inspector, so it's no surprise, is it, that I married a liar?"

"Leta!"

She raised her chin as her father came into the room. "Yes, Daddy?"

"You should lie down, rest."

Leta Halstead shrugged, slid off the divan and walked with a loose-hipped stride to the corridor that obviously led to the bedrooms. She paused to turn back and say with a sardonic smile, "I'll come downtown and make a statement, Inspector. After I'm rested."

Perry Alaric waited until she had disappeared before saying, "The doctor's given her sedatives. I thought she was okay, but as you can see, she's rather confused about everything."

"Confused in what way?" asked Bourke.

A shade of vexation crossed Alaric's blunt features. "My wife should be here any moment. She's been making the funeral arrangements. She can explain about Leta much better than I."

He checked his watch, grunted, and said, "Can I get you something? Coffee perhaps?"

"Thank you, no. If I could just ask a few questions..."

Alaric looked at Carol with heavy surprise. "You want to question *me*? I assure you I don't know the first thing about Brin's death. I assume that he disturbed some petty thief, who panicked and killed him." Belatedly he added, "It's a terrible thing."

"When did you last see your son-in-law?"

"The day before yesterday. We had lunch."

Bourke said, "And you discussed...?"

Alaric looked disgusted to be asked the question. "Nothing relevant to this, I assure you. Just general business and family matters. Things of that nature."

Carol was resigned to fighting every step of the way to get information from the man, so she was taken aback when he sat down on the divan Leta had vacated and said, "Let me tell you about Brin and Leta."

He sat forward, dangling his thick hands between his knees. "I was bloody relieved when a man like Brin Halstead took an interest in Leta. Maybe her mother and I have spoiled her, but she's never been steady. Leta's clever enough, but she was always taking up with men who used her badly. I couldn't have been happier when she and Brin married. Thought it'd be the making of her, but it didn't work out the way I expected. She became aggressive, accused Brin of lying to her. It was nonsense, of course, and I told her so, but Leta's never taken my advice. Too often she seems to go off in the opposite direction."

Carol hadn't been expecting this soul-searching from a man like Perry Alaric, particularly in front of two strangers. She thought of Leta's words, *I come from a family of liars.* Perhaps this was what she meant.

The front door opened, and Iniga Alaric entered. In one glance she seemed to take in the situation and act on it. She deposited her things on a marble-topped table near the entrance and came rushing over.

"Perry, darling!" She pecked his cheek. "You've offered no refreshments. I'm sure these police officers would appreciate *something.* How about coffee? I can tell you, if no one else wants a cup, *I* do."

Having dispatched him to the kitchen, she turned a charming smile on Bourke and Carol. "Honestly, men have *no* idea, do they?" Her smile faded. "This is such a tragic time." Her face conveyed the requisite grief, but Carol wasn't convinced that she was feeling any genuine sense of loss.

If Iniga Alaric remembered meeting Carol previously, she gave no sign of it. She sat down, smoothed the skirt of her lavender linen dress, and fixed them with an expectant look. Her dark blond hair was styled elegantly, her face perfectly made up, her feet in Italian leather shoes precisely placed side by side.

Carol introduced herself and Bourke. Iniga Alaric acknowledged this with a gracious nod. "Have you seen Leta?" she asked.

"Only for a short time," said Bourke.

Her husband, from the doorway, said, "I had to send her to lie down again. It was clear she was too upset to continue the interview." He came over to place on a low brass table a tray containing delicate china cups, a cream jug, and a sugar bowl. "I'll get the coffee."

"Poor Leta," said Iniga Alaric, watching her husband leave the room. "She's like her father. She takes things very hard."

Carol fought off an impulse to make some sardonic remark about how having a husband die a violent death could be expected to be upsetting; instead she contented herself by mentioning that it was essential that the interview be completed as soon as possible.

"Leta won't have to identify the body?" This thought appeared to alarm Iniga Alaric more than the sudden death of her son-in-law.

"A visual identification would not be appropriate," said Carol.

The meaning wasn't lost on Leta's mother. "I see, of course, the fire . . ." ·

Carol visualized the corpse's head. Even without the blaze, the face would have been unrecognizable. "We will be asking your daughter to identify personal effects — a watch, wallet, things like that."

Iniga Alaric leaned forward, hands clasped in her

lap. "Brin wore a wedding ring that Leta had designed for him. Very heavy gold, embossed. And a Rolex watch. That was a present from me."

"These will all be returned," said Bourke, "but there may be some damage from the heat."

"The fire." She gave a little shake of her head, lifting her shoulders as she did so. "One can hardly imagine the type of miscreant who would do such a thing. I mean, I can understand some desperate creature breaking into a medical facility in search of drugs. But murder. Just to calmly kill someone and then set a fire."

Carol glanced at Bourke. He said, "There's no evidence of a break-in."

"What are you saying? That it wasn't some drug addict?" Iniga Alaric seemed genuinely puzzled. "But we've been told it was arson." Indignation bubbled to the surface, and her voice grew louder as she exclaimed, "Surely you're not suggesting that Brin had anything to do with it?"

"At this early stage we're gathering as much information as possible," Carol said.

Apparently appeased, Iniga Alaric murmured, "Of course."

"When did you last speak with Dr. Halstead?"

"We had a family dinner last weekend, on Sunday night at our place. Poor Brin, he was so enthusiastic about the future."

"Did he seem worried about anything?"

Bourke's question seemed to offend her. "If he had been worried about something, I would have noticed. We were very close." She gave him a little nod, as if to put him in his place, then raised her voice to call, "Perry, we're waiting for the coffee."

45

On cue, Perry Alaric appeared with a graceful coffeepot decorated with the same delicate spray of bamboo as the china setting. Under his wife's critical gaze, he busied himself pouring and distributing the coffee. Carol noticed he didn't provide one for himself.

"Darling," said Iniga Alaric, "will you join us?"

"I don't think so. If you'll excuse me, I want to make sure Leta's all right."

"Leta *is* fragile," said his wife after he had left the room. She took a small sip from her cup. "And so, despite appearances, is my husband."

Her expression indicating she was about to entrust Carol with something personal, she went on, "I don't suppose you know, Inspector, but my son — our son — was taken from us two years ago next month, not long after Brin and Leta were married. Frankly, I don't think Perry has ever recovered from the blow. It was an accident, a dreadful accident, and I don't blame Leta for it at all. She lost control of the car — it was wet, stormy, so I can see how it could happen with just a moment's inattention. Perhaps she was lighting a cigarette ..."

She paused for a moment, then went on, "The car — it was a wedding present from Perry, which somehow made it so much worse — rolled three times. It was a miracle Leta was spared. Of course, she *was* wearing a seat belt, though, unaccountably, Conrad was not. He was thrown from the car and injured terribly. He never regained consciousness. We had a vigil around his bed, and when the time came I said 'Turn off the life support,' and my son died there in my arms."

There was silence. In her mind Carol ran through

appropriate responses and came up empty. She was saved by Bourke, who said with sympathy, "Losing a child must be a devastating experience."

With a jolt, Carol recalled that Bourke was speaking from personal knowledge. Long before she had known him, he had lost both his wife and child in a boating accident.

"I see you understand," said Iniga Alaric to Bourke. "That means you will also understand why, for Perry's sake, we are going to have another child — a boy."

She paused — for effect, Carol was sure — then continued, "Dear, dear, Brin. It was he who persuaded us to go ahead with it. I won't go into details, but suffice to say that a surrogate mother will be bearing our son just after Christmas."

Twenty minutes later, descending in the miniature lift, Bourke said to Carol, "Why do I feel that we've just been guest stars in an episode of a soap opera?"

"Not stars," said Carol. "I think we were supposed to be the gullible audience."

CHAPTER FIVE

The roads were congested and the drivers more than usually truculent, so it took longer than usual to travel from the rarefied luxury of the Halstead residence with its sensational view of the harbor to Carol's humdrum office with an aspect that largely consisted of the wall of a neighboring building.

While Bourke drove with neat economy, unruffled by the heavy traffic, Carol studied the picture Iniga Alaric had reluctantly provided from her daughter's photo album. Brin Halstead wasn't conventionally handsome, but he had a crooked, little-boy smile that showed excellent teeth. He was wearing obviously expensive casual clothes that showed his athletic body to advantage. On his left hand the wedding ring his mother-in-law had mentioned caught the light.

What had he been thinking when this photograph was taken? She turned it over. On the back was scrawled a date that indicated it had been taken six months before and the notation *At Keith's.*

Carol put the photo away and spent the rest of the time discussing Bourke's pending meeting with Glen Daris, the man who had recently sued Halstead over the fertility treatment Daris and his wife had received.

Anne Newsome greeted Carol at the office door. "I've got a message from Dr. Vail. He says that the inventory will take him all today and most of tomorrow, and that you'll need a court order to get access to any confidential files." She chuckled. "Little bantam rooster of a guy, isn't he? I saw him in action at the clinic this afternoon, bouncing everyone around — or trying to."

"Did you notice Gilda Milton?"

"Dr. Halstead's personal assistant? Yes, she was nice. Got coffee and doughnuts organized for everyone."

"I'd like to see her tomorrow. Would you arrange it, please?"

Anne nodded. "She's just the sort that people tell their troubles to," she said. "I suppose every office has one. A sort of mother figure."

"And who's the mother figure here?" asked Carol facetiously.

"That would be me," said Maureen Oatland from the doorway. "I've always fancied myself in that role."

With notepad under one arm, she sauntered in, munching a pastry. It was a standing joke that Maureen had a personal junk-food detector, and if there was an outlet peddling cholesterol-loaded substances anywhere near a crime scene, she would find it.

Anne smirked at Maureen's self-description, made a derisive comment, and took herself off. She put her head back around the edge of the door to say, "Oh, and Dr. Vail said that any leaks to the media would be coming from *us,* not his staff."

"His staff?" said Carol to Maureen. "I wonder who actually owns the clinic now."

"And I'm the very woman to tell you." Maureen settled her large frame into a chair. "The clinic is owned by a holding company, with Brin Halstead the majority shareholder and Halstead's wife and William Vail dividing up the remainder."

She gestured with the remains of the pastry. "Want one? I've got a bag of them outside."

Although tempted — all Carol had consumed was a hastily gulped sandwich at lunchtime — she refused the offer. She wanted to concentrate on work. "You've already got some financial details? That was quick."

"Wonderful what you can do with a computer, a telephone, and a persuasive manner," said Maureen, slapping the notepad on the desk. "Just preliminary stuff, but basically Halstead's in debt to his eyebrows, which is a little surprising, since I gather he charges sky-high fees for his services and that the seriously rich don't mind at all, as long as the results are there."

She referred to her notes. "This month in his personal finances he was already past due on his home mortgage, and his credit cards are at the max. As far as his company, fetchingly called Halstead Procreative Services, is concerned, he was trying to renegotiate terms so that payments on the building and equipment would be delayed until next year."

"Who were his creditors?"

"A mix of financial institutions. There's also a suggestion that his mother-in-law has been very generous."

"Iniga Alaric? How generous?"

Maureen shrugged. "They were personal, unsecured loans — or perhaps straight-out gifts, so there's no formal record. I'll see what I can find out, but I've got the impression it was a lot of money."

It was possible, Carol thought, in the light of Iniga Alaric's revelation about a surrogate bearing a new son for the family, that this generosity might be a payback.

She said, "I want to know if there's been any un-usual pattern of withdrawals from Halstead's accounts lately."

Maureen gave her a shrewd look. "Blackmail?"

"Only a thought. He might be strapped for cash for some other reason — gambling or drugs, for example."

Heaving herself up, Maureen said, "I'll see what I can find out." She brushed crumbs off her wrinkled brown slacks. "And I suppose you'd like the details of Halstead's will, too."

"I suppose I would," said Carol.

"I'll bring you back coffee and a pastry." Maureen made a face at her. "That's what we motherly types do."

With the guilty thought that she still hadn't

checked how David had gone at his school sports day,
Carol picked up the receiver. She promised herself —
and she'd promise David — that she'd make time for
him this weekend, no matter how pressing her
caseload.

"Eleanor? It's Carol again. Is David home yet?
How did he go in his races?"

"It's a shame, Carol, but you've just missed him.
Justin decided to take David and a bunch of his
friends down to McDonald's to celebrate with ham-
burgers."

"Justin in *McDonald's*?" Carol had trouble
visualizing her very correct, barrister ex-husband in
such a place.

Eleanor laughed. "Hard to imagine, isn't it? But
he did make a firm commitment — David made him
swear on a Bible — that if David won, he could have
any treat he wanted."

"So he did win?"

"Yes, two races, and a second in another. He's so
excited. I'll let him tell you all the details himself."

Carol promised to call back later and broke the
connection. She liked Eleanor very much, and in
different circumstances, she believed that they could
have been friends. But Justin Hart had made anything of that sort impossible. After his initial
white-hot anger at the breakup of his and Carol's
marriage, where he had threatened crushing legal
battles over the custody of David, he had retreated
into a cool, distant politeness. Carol was the biological mother of his son, and that gave her certain
rights. In his lawyerly way, he made sure that she
was treated fairly, and never denied access, but their
rare conversations were conducted with chilly civility.

Carol checked her watch. Sybil should be home. She punched the familiar number and listened to the phone at the other end of the line ring. Shutting her eyes, she could imagine the sound filling the rooms of Sybil's light-filled house perched high above the beach. The sea would be so blue it almost hurt the eyes, and the thump of surf hitting the beach, the sound of the ocean's heartbeat, would be blown by the breeze.

After four rings, Sybil's recorded voice cut in. Carol left a brief message that she'd try again, and hung up, feeling somehow abandoned. She had to smile at herself: Two phone calls without the person being available hardly constituted wholesale rejection.

Carol was making a face at a mouthful of cold coffee she'd absentmindedly taken when Anne brought in several faxed sheets. "From Gilda Milton," she said. "A Halstead Clinic staff list and Dr. Halstead's Wednesday schedule."

Carol glanced at the staff list and put it to one side. She looked at the faxed page of Halstead's appointment book with more immediate interest. In neat, rounded handwriting, someone — almost certainly Gilda — had given more details for each entry. At eight in the morning Halstead had been at his dentist's office. *Six-month teeth cleaning,* was the annotation. The name *Lorant* appeared at ten-thirty with the note, *Tom Lorant — staff.* At twelve Halstead had apparently gone to lunch with someone called Cindy Farr. Next to her name was the intriguing word *surrogate.* The afternoon was blank until a name Carol recognized was written in for three-thirty. Noelle Winthall was a journalist, and a good one. Carol had met her a couple of times when Noelle had been doing a series of articles on women in the police force. That made it all the more interesting to see the explanation *client* written next to her name.

Leta Halstead had said her husband spoke of a meeting with colleagues at some city hotel on Wednesday evening, but the three-thirty appointment was the last one listed for the day.

Bourke came in, shirtsleeves rolled up and tie loosened. "Long day," he said around a yawn. "You should go home."

Carol passed the pages to Bourke. "Gilda Milton provided this staff list, plus a schedule of Halstead's Wednesday appointments. I must say she's rather more helpful than Dr. Vail."

"Ah, Gilda," said Bourke, grinning.

"So you've been using the famous Mark Bourke charm again?"

"Again," he agreed. "She's a nice woman. I like her, so it was no effort to chat to her this morning while we were following Vail around. He sent Lorant off to check the basement again, and Gilda and I cooled our heels while the good doctor tut-tutted his way through what was left of the office that was torched. Talking to her, I'd say she has a better idea of how the place runs than he does."

"So what did you get?"

He rubbed one eye with his knuckles. "Just bits and pieces. One thing, though — Halstead was actively recruiting clients in the gay community. Gilda says he was targeting gay male couples, who wanted the whole surrogate mother bit handled on a business level, and lesbians, who wanted sperm certified free of problems, such as HIV."

"That reminds me. We need that list of clients from Vail."

"I'll lean on him a little," said Bourke. "He's all bluff. A bit of pressure, and he'll crumble."

Carol was diverted for a moment by the picture of Bourke leaning on the diminutive Dr. Vail. Bourke went on, "Gilda also mentioned that Halstead was in the process of setting up what he called a *Genius Register* that only held frozen sperm taken from donors who had superior abilities, such as a very high IQ, or were outstanding sportsmen or musicians or whatever."

He yawned again, stretching his arms and loosening his shoulders. "Got to get home to Pat. I promised her I'd try not to be too late."

"Before you go, what happened with Daris, the guy who was suing Halstead?"

"Glen Daris agreed to see me at short notice and at some inconvenience to him, as he and his family are about to leave on an overseas holiday. When we met, he couldn't have been easier to get along with. He answered all my questions — there's a gag order on the actual amount of the settlement, of course."

Carol hadn't had time to check the details of the case, but she and Bourke had discussed the broad outline, as it had received very wide publicity. "Daris claimed that the baby his wife carried wasn't genetically related to either of them. That's right, isn't it?"

"Yes. It started when Daris and his wife, Leigh, had trouble conceiving. They're both in their late thirties, so they went for counseling to the Halstead Clinic. Brin Halstead convinced them the only chance of a viable pregnancy was in-vitro fertilization, using Leigh's eggs and Daris's sperm. So they went ahead and were absolutely thrilled after only a few tries to find that they were expecting a baby."

He tilted his head. "Odd, isn't it, that the suspicion that he wasn't related to them would have come up in the first place. I mean, the little boy was perfectly healthy, so why go to the expense of a DNA profile?"

"You think someone from the clinic told them?"

"Daris said it was all his wife's idea. She felt something was wrong." He darted a mischievous look at her. "A sterling example of women's intuition in action."

Refusing to rise to the bait, Carol said, "I presume Daris confronted Halstead?"

"He did, and Halstead denied everything. Said the DNA results were faulty and that the child was theirs. I think he was gambling that because Daris isn't rich, he wouldn't have the money to pursue the matter, but he underestimated the man. Of course Halstead's insurance company paid in the end, but the facts that the case got to court and that some juicy details were fed to the media meant very bad publicity for the clinic."

"Alibis?"

"For Wednesday evening? Yes, I checked it out, since Daris and his wife are flying out tonight and extradition is such a business. There was a family going-away party last night, with a score of witnesses who'll place them there."

Suddenly curious, Carol said, "What happened to the baby? Are they keeping him?"

"Little Matthew? They certainly are. Daris showed me a couple of photos, and it's obvious he's loved. He said they've come to look upon him as adopted, and that's what they'll tell him when he's older."

Carol bleakly considered the contents of her refrigerator while Sinker shrieked to indicate that collapse from starvation was a real possibility since it was eleven o'clock at night and she had just got home. Then, with an artful duplicity that Carol could only admire, he maneuvered himself so she accidentally stepped on his tail, allowing him to add outrage at her cruelty to the list of her crimes.

He took his black-and-white body to a strategic position near his bowl and sat gazing at her with a look that implied that he would not be surprised if she picked him up and drop-kicked him next.

"You miss Jeffrey, don't you?" she said, though, to be honest, it was Carol who really missed Jeffrey's ginger face and loud, bubbling purr. Sinker was quite content to be the center of Carol's attention and to be relieved from the trying necessity of eating everything in his food bowl at one sitting in order to prevent Jeffrey from finishing it off.

The phone rang as Carol located a can of cat food, a deluxe variety that Sinker favored, at least for the moment. Rummaging in the drawer for an opener, she tucked the receiver between her shoulder and jaw. "Yes? Oh darling, I'd tried to get you earlier.

You got my message? I'm going to be tied up with a case, but Saturday night's still on."

"I've just seen you on television," said Sybil, "walking around a svelte building looking as if you owned it."

Carol suddenly wanted to see Sybil here, now, in the kitchen beside her. That was impossible, of course, so she said, "I could come over, even though it's late."

"I'd love it, but be practical. It's nearly midnight, and by the time you get here and we talk, and ..."

"It's that last *and* that I'm interested in," Carol said.

Sybil laughed. "Saturday," she said. "How early can you get here?"

"As soon as I can, but I won't have a definite time until I see how tomorrow and Saturday work out. I'll call you."

They talked for a few minutes about various things, Carol telling Sybil what a track star David was turning out to be. She could hear the pride in her voice as she said it and hoped that David had also heard that pleasure in his achievements when she had finally got him on the phone before she left the office.

Before Sybil hung up, Carol said, "I love you. I really do."

Sybil's reply, "Me too," was unsatisfying, although Carol wasn't quite sure why. After she had replaced the receiver, Carol spent a long moment staring at the phone, as if it had an answer to her dilemma. She rubbed her forehead, feeling a fatigue headache starting.

On the way home she'd seen Christmas decorations, and some of the neighborhood houses already had lights strung through trees. On Christmas day she usually had a barbecue here in the garden, with glimpses of water and birds calling and the hot summer sun shining. It wouldn't happen this year.

"Problems, problems," she said to Sinker, who was gobbling his food in a manner designed to show he thought she might snatch it from him at any moment. "Emotional blackmail. You and Sybil know all about it."

Immediately she felt ashamed to have put into words something so unfair. "Sorry," she said to the cat, knowing that her apology was to Sybil.

CHAPTER SIX

Crisp was the first word that came to Carol's mind when Professor Joan Yaller welcomed them into her university office early Friday morning. A tiny woman, she didn't come to Carol's shoulder, but she was resolutely stiff backed and held her head high. She had a firm, fast handshake and a concise welcoming smile for each of them.

"Inspector Ashton. Sergeant Bourke. How can I help you?"

As she and Bourke took the proffered seats, Carol

glanced around. She imagined that Bourke felt right at home, as the room was austerely furnished and tidy to the point of anonymity. There were no photographs or paintings, and the books on the metal shelves were precisely aligned and marshaled, Carol was sure, in some esoteric academic order.

Professor Yaller seated herself, leaned her elbows on the immaculate surface of her spotless desk, linked her fingers, and directed an unspoken inquiry in their direction.

"Dr. Brin Halstead," said Carol. "He died on Wednesday night."

"Murdered, I believe. At least, that's what the media are saying. Is it accurate?"

Bourke said, "Quite possibly."

"We need background in the type of genetic work he would have been doing at his clinic," said Carol.

Professor Yaller pursed her lips. "I must say here, Inspector, that I heartily disliked the man — our paths crossed now and then — but that said, I must admit that he was a brilliant technician. Indeed, the popular description of the Halstead Clinic as being at the cutting edge of genetics has some truth in it."

"Do you know Halstead's partner, Dr. Vail?" asked Bourke.

"Bill Vail? His *junior* partner, I think you'll find. Brin Halstead never did like to be overshadowed, so he chose a colleague who was quite competent, but able to be intimidated. You'll find Bill Vail's bark is a great deal less than his bite." The professor gave a frosty smile. "Although I wouldn't say the same about Bill's wife. I don't imagine you've met Ursula, as yet, but I think you'll find her ... interesting."

Deciding not to get offtrack by pursuing this intriguing remark, Carol said, "Could you give us a general idea of what is done at the Halstead Clinic?"

Professor Yaller settled back in her chair, obviously in teacher mode. "A sizable number of couples have trouble conceiving, and this is exacerbated by the tendency of young women to put off having their families until quite late in their reproductive lives. I'm sure you're familiar with in-vitro fertilization, which essentially is where an egg removed from a donor's ovary is united in a petri dish with sperm from a selected male partner. Actually, to maximize the chances, multiple eggs are fertilized, and selected growing embryos are implanted in the mother's — or a surrogate's — womb."

As though uncomfortable, Bourke shifted in his chair. "The success rate's quite high, isn't it?"

"IVF procedures have certainly been refined since the first test-tube baby in 1978. But there are many failures, and quite a high proportion of women never conceive. Others have to endure the procedure repeatedly to get a viable pregnancy."

Carol suddenly felt the privilege of her own life. She had married on schedule, had conceived at an appropriate time, and, without difficulty had been delivered of a healthy child nine months later. Her thoughts strayed to David — she must call him again, persuade him to make a little time for her this weekend. The irony wasn't lost on Carol — too often she had slotted him into her life when it was convenient, but now it was David who was having problems fitting *her* into his busy schedule.

"Of course," the professor was saying, "the fertility clinics fail to mention that this is an expensive, stressful, and emotionally exhausting experience for a couple, especially for the woman."

Bourke seemed about to ask something, but shook his head and remained silent. Carol had a moment's curiosity, but her attention switched back to Joan Yaller as the professor said, "Brin Halstead saw himself at the frontier of fertility science. He certainly was involved in postmenopausal pregnancy, using hormones to prepare an older woman's body, long past the age one would consider normal for childbearing, for implantation from a young egg donor."

"I can't imagine why a woman would want to do that," said Bourke. "By the time the kid was a teenager, the mother could be in her seventies."

Professor Yaller gave him a dry smile. "I think you'll find that there has always been a considerable number of *fathers* in their seventies or eighties with teenage children."

From his expression, Carol could see that Bourke had decided not to get into this particular debate. He turned to a new page in his notebook. "And other procedures?" he said.

"I know that he's had a considerable number of inquiries about delayed conception. This is where a woman has her eggs harvested and frozen when she is young and the quality of her eggs is high. Implantation will occur much later when her career is established. She may even decide not to bear the child herself but to use a surrogate mother."

"Would it be Dr. Halstead's role to recruit surrogate mothers?" Carol asked.

"In some cases the client would have someone in mind, perhaps a sister or relative or some other person willing and able to carry and bear the child. There have been custody battles in the past, when the surrogate mother decided not to give up the child, so Brin Halstead favored what one might call professional surrogates who have a contractual arrangement with the clinic and the future parents. I'm aware of several young women that have had more than one pregnancy for different patients of his."

"They'd have to be well paid!" said Bourke with feeling.

"I imagine they are," said the professor, amused. "This is an interesting legal issue, and, as with many fertility procedures, the science is outstripping the law. For instance, another area Halstead may have been exploring is parenthood for dead donors. It's possible, for example, to take viable sperm from a man after death, in some instances considerably more than twenty-four hours later, and freeze the sample for later use. I'm sure you can see the problems that could arise with inheritance, for example, if the father is legally dead when the sperm are removed."

She paused and then went on, "I've also heard that Halstead has tried transplanting ovaries from aborted fetuses into aging women, but I stress I have no evidence for this. The ethics of the procedure, and the problems of rejection by the recipient, probably make it impossible, at least at present."

Carol said, "We've been told there have been rumors that Dr. Halstead was involved in cloning."

"The government has proscribed cloning, as I'm sure you're aware."

Carol gave her an amused glance. "Well, that would be the end of it then!"

Professor Yaller smiled in turn. "Of course it wouldn't. Scientists always want to push the envelope, and cloning is no longer the exclusive realm of popular science fantasy. With animals, it's becoming almost commonplace."

"I thought there was some difficulty with human beings," said Bourke, frowning, "and that it wouldn't work, the way it did with that sheep in Scotland."

"The famous Dolly? Well, there are difficulties, but none insurmountable. In fact, recent experiments in America have been successful in cloning different species, including monkeys. One experiment created viable embryos using cow eggs as incubators. The challenge now is not so much cloning but bringing a cloned embryo to full development."

Bourke looked appalled. "Wouldn't this sort of thing create monsters?"

"Not at all. The nucleus containing the DNA is the key. When it's introduced into the egg, it is the blueprint, if you will, of the animal to be."

"Or the person," said Carol, "if we're talking about human cloning."

Joan Yaller's face grew more animated as she said, "It really is the most fascinating prospect. Do you realize that once the technology is fully established, in theory anyone can be cloned without the person's permission, or even knowledge?"

"Oh, brave new world," said Bourke, uncharacteristically sardonic.

"What's required is a healthy cell, and we give

those off all the time. A dentist, for example, could harvest cells from your mouth, and each one would contain your full DNA genetic blueprint. Then, in theory, all that's needed is an ovum — an egg — and a womb."

"It can't be that easy."

"It isn't, of course. In very simple terms, the original cell has to be placed in a sort of suspended animation, to hold the DNA ready. Then the egg that is to receive it must have its nucleus, which contains its own DNA, removed. The cell and the egg are placed together and fused with either a jolt of electricity or a chemical signal, which tricks the egg into thinking it's been fertilized by a sperm. This starts the process of division. There's an extremely high failure rate at this stage, but with multiple attempts, at least a few may start to grow into embryos, which can then be implanted in a surrogate mother's womb."

Carol asked several more questions, and while the professor elaborated, Carol noticed that Bourke was fidgeting in his chair. This was so unusual that after they had thanked Joan Yaller and taken their leave, Carol felt constrained to say, as they walked to the car, "What's the matter?"

Bourke looked at her sideways. "Nothing."

"Mark, come on."

"Carol, I haven't said anything, but..."

She stopped walking and turned to face him. "Is something wrong?"

"Not exactly." He looked down at the ground. "Fact is, Pat and I want to start a family, and we found there was a bit of a problem. We've been going to a fertility clinic for months, so far without success."

"Not Halstead Clinic?" Carol said involuntarily.

Bourke's lips twitched. "Thank God, no. Nothing to do with him."

As they resumed walking, Carol wondered why he hadn't told her before. Then she wondered, uncomfortably, why she would have expected him to share this most intimate part of his marriage.

She had an aversion to the morgue, to its pervasive smell of disinfectants and preservatives that could never quite overcome the stench of death. Carol always left the building with a feeling of relief. She'd endured the commitment to be there and, unchanged, walked out into the ordinary, mundane world.

That wasn't quite true, of course. She had a memory of some poet's words from her English classes so long ago — John Donne, she thought. She recalled that he'd written something about how each death of a person diminished him. That was how she felt when she left a postmortem — diminished, modified, reduced in some way.

Brin Halstead's postmortem had been a test of her fortitude. Along with the usual smells was something else — charred flesh. Being burned alive was something that particularly horrified Carol. She never examined the reasons why she should have an extreme reaction to the concept, although, dimly, she seemed to remember from her childhood a neighbor pulled screaming from a house, clothes afire.

The pathologist, Jeff Duke, had been as brutally cheerful as always. "Have a look at the X rays," he'd said. "Someone bashed the bejesus out of him. Smashed his teeth and jaw, caved in his skull."

"Would it need a man's strength?"

"No. One lucky blow to disable him — his fingers aren't broken, so he didn't try to defend himself — and you could take any number of good swings at his skull."

Thinking of Ursula Vail and of Leta Halstead, Carol said, "How about a slightly-built woman?"

"This is an equal-opportunity murder, Carol. Any reasonably fit woman, using two-handed blows, could have done the damage, if she put her back into it."

Carol had examined the X rays displayed on the lighted panel with close attention, wanting an excuse not to look at the grotesque corpse on the table. "His front teeth are shattered. Will that make dental identification hard?"

"A little more difficult, but it shouldn't make much difference. Short of destroying both jaws, you can't obliterate the unique root patterns, even if you use a pair of pliers to wrench out the teeth themselves."

Carol had spent enough time staring at the light panel. She straightened her shoulders under the protective paper gown she was wearing. "What's your best guess at a weapon?"

"Iron bar, maybe. Come and have a look."

Carol made it a point of honor never to show revulsion or squeamishness. This was for her personal standing with her colleagues and for her self-respect, but also because she felt each victim deserved her professional regard.

She'd seen the typical aggressive appearance of a badly burned body several times before. Halstead's knees were flexed, his heels touching the surface of the table as though he wished to propel himself upright. His elbows were bent, his clenched hands raised toward the ceiling. Carol knew that the heat had caused the contraction of muscles and sinews, but she couldn't help feeling that Brin Halstead had met his death with defiance and anger.

"No soot in the lungs. He was dead before the fire."

This was a comfort. It was almost too terrible to consider the pain and terror of being cooked alive. I'm getting soft, she'd thought, watching Duke fillet the remains, chatting as he did so.

Peering into the gaping abdominal cavity, he said, "You say he had a meal around seven-thirty, eight?"

"So his wife says. Spaghetti and meat sauce."

"Not much for a last meal, eh?" said Duke. "And not all that much help. Time of death calculated by digestion of stomach contents is notably unreliable, but I'll do my best."

Carol went out into the ordinary world and looked at ordinary people walking by. For a moment she envied them all. They had no idea, no imaginative concept, of what happened behind these anonymous walls. No images to pounce on them in dreams.

CHAPTER SEVEN

A cleanup was going on at the Halstead Clinic when Carol arrived. Although the laboratory where Halstead died was still off-limits, Carol had agreed that the clinic could open for business. A platoon of cleaners were working to get the floor of the entrance lobby back to its previous pristine whiteness and to clean the residue of smoke from walls and glass surfaces.

It was very chilly inside, as the air-conditioning was obviously on full in an attempt to keep the stink of smoke and burned material at bay. On the top floor she was relieved to find that the smell was noticeably less.

"He kept all his appointments in this," said Gilda Milton, handing Carol a blue leather-bound book. "Brin wrote it up himself and just told me the ones he needed to be reminded about."

Carol flipped it open to the Wednesday Halstead had died. Although she hadn't realized it from the faxed copy, all the entries were made in soft, dark pencil. She narrowed her eyes, tilting the book. "Has something been rubbed out here?"

"Let me see." Gilda stared at the page. "I see what you mean. Looks like an initial next to seven o'clock. What do you think? Maybe a *U*?"

Although she immediately thought of Ursula Vail, Carol said offhandedly, "Probably nothing. I'll have a look at it later."

"Anything else I can do for you?"

"What was Dr. Halstead like?" said Carol.

Gilda Milton considered the question. "You've seen photos, I suppose. Brin had a sort of ugly-attractive face. He smiled a lot, and had a warm, oozy voice that made for a good bedside manner." She smiled at Carol. "This the sort of thing you want?"

"Anything you want to say."

Carol leaned back in her chair. They were in the sitting area outside Halstead's opulent office. *Opulent,* she thought, was the right word. Everything seemed to be chosen to ostentatiously trumpet wealth, to impress with conspicuous consumption. It didn't work for Carol. There were too many shiny things, too much gilt, too many paintings crowding the walls.

Gilda Milton looked serene, but she was drumming her plump fingers on the brocade arm of her chair. Carol considered her dispassionately. Comfortably curved rather than overweight, she had a pleasant face, pale, intelligent eyes, and wavy, badly-styled hair of an indeterminate brown.

"Brin looked after his appearance," she said. Her manner was impersonal, as though she were reporting on some acquaintance and not the boss she had worked closely with for the past five years. "He was thin, had a nice body and broad shoulders, and wore good clothes. Had straight brown hair that he let fall boyishly over one eye. And he could be *very* charming."

Amused by this cool assessment, Carol said, "You didn't altogether approve?"

"Of what? The whole Halstead package? I liked working for him — it was interesting, and he paid me well."

They discussed her duties as his personal assistant for a few moments, and then Carol said, "I've been looking through the staff list you faxed to me yesterday. Did Dr. Halstead have problems with anyone in particular?"

"Enough to kill him, you mean? Brin was very demanding, so he wasn't easy to work for. There was some friction over that."

"Actually," said Carol, "I was thinking of someone leaking damaging material to the media."

"Elaine Kaynes," said Gilda.

"Why her?"

"I caught Elaine photocopying confidential stuff, and I told Brin about it."

"When was this?"

"It was last Friday. A week ago today."

"Tell me about her."

Gilda gave Carol a comfortable smile. "Elaine's head of the nursing staff, and very good at her job. But she's one of those people who're never satisfied. She always has to pick at things, find something wrong. I'm sure you know the sort."

Bourke had said that he liked Gilda Milton, that she was nice, but Carol was starting to pick up a hint of smugness, of conceited self-assurance. Carol said, "Dr. Halstead trusted your judgment."

It was a statement, not a question, and it pleased Gilda Milton. "He did. Implicitly."

"So he would have shared with you details of the direction in which the clinic was going."

Gilda straightened in her chair. "I'm not sure I understand what you mean, Inspector."

"If Elaine Kaynes is the person approaching the media, she claims to have evidence about human cloning."

"Here in the clinic? Research of that type, surely, is under government purview."

"So you have no personal knowledge of anything to do with cloning?"

Gilda spread her hands. "Personally, no. I can't be responsible for what some clients might have thought, reading between the lines."

"Dr. Halstead implied something, without actually saying it?"

"Cruel, really," said Gilda, "to raise their hopes." She leaned forward, smiling, the picture of someone about to confide a secret. "The lesbians and the gays," she said. "Cloning's the way they want to go."

* * * * *

73

Carol found Thomas Lorant down in the basement wearing a heavy apron and thick gloves. He closed the lid of the liquid nitrogen container and stripped off his protective gear. "Just going through every item, one by one," he said, indicating a clipboard. "In spite of what Bill Vail says, I don't think anything's been taken."

"Could they have been changed around?"

Lorant looked at Carol with surprise. "Wrongly labeled, you mean?"

"Something like that."

He chuckled softly. "What an ingenious mind you have, Inspector."

Standing near him, she was aware that he was even taller than she had supposed. He stood quietly, his hands relaxed, with a pensive expression, waiting for her to say something further.

"You had an appointment to see Dr. Halstead on Wednesday morning."

"Yes, that's right." He smoothed his mustache with a forefinger. "Ten-thirty."

"What did you discuss?"

Carol thought for a moment he might refuse to answer, but then he said, "To use the right jargon, my career path. I wanted to know what sort of future I had here."

"And?"

He raised his eyebrows fractionally. "Brin was very reassuring. He said he valued my work and that I could expect a substantial increase in my salary."

Thinking of the financial trouble Halstead had been in, Carol said, "Was this to take effect immediately?"

"Not immediately. At the beginning of next year."

There was something wrong, Carol thought. She had no reason other than instinct to think it, but she was sure Thomas Lorant wasn't being entirely truthful.

"When was the last time you saw Dr. Halstead?"

He gave her a slow smile. "You know, I've read that phrase in mystery novels so many times, but I never expected to be asked the question."

"And the answer?"

"I'm sorry, Inspector, I'm not trying to play games with you. I spoke with Brin at five about ordering medical supplies. I never saw him again."

"I'm about to make your day," said Carol, "by asking you another question from a crime novel. Do you know anyone who'd want to hurt Dr. Halstead?"

Lorant grinned at her question. "Lots," he said. "That is to say, this whole field of fertility treatment is a minefield of emotions. People get very disappointed when things don't work out, and the failure rate is high."

"Anyone in particular?"

He smoothed his mustache again. "Not with the patients, exactly. Brin's been having a bit of trouble with one of our surrogates, Cindy Farr, or rather, her brother, Howie."

"What sort of trouble?"

"Well," said Lorant, "I was in Brin's office last week when Howie turned up, red in the face and swearing. When I was leaving the room I heard Howie say he was going to bash Brin's head in."

* * * * *

75

Before she started the car, Carol used her cellular phone. The number was a direct line to Madeline at the television station, so Carol wasn't surprised when Madeline answered it herself. "Carol! I was just thinking of you. Is this business or pleasure?"

"Is Elaine Kaynes your source at the Halstead Clinic?"

"You know I can't —"

"Madeline, just answer me."

After a pause, Madeline said, "Yes."

"And *The Shipley Report* is paying her?"

"Reasonable expenses only."

"How good's the material she's brought you?"

"Good. Convincing."

"And you've got other people to back up her story?"

"Well . . . I may have." Madeline was obviously unhappy the way the conversation was going.

"Okay, I want their names. And don't bullshit me, Madeline. This is a murder case."

Bourke was deep in paperwork when she looked in on him. "Mark, check out a surrogate mother called Cindy Farr that the clinic's been using. Her brother, Howie, was in Halstead's office the Friday of last week, threatening to bash in Halstead's brains."

"I bet he's sorry he said that," said Bourke, noting the name.

"And here's Halstead's personal appointment book," she said, handing it to him. "Check it out for names, patterns of appointments, anything that looks out of place. If he was broke because he was paying a bookie or a blackmailer, there might be something to indicate it there."

As he took it from her she added, "Look at seven o'clock on Wednesday. It looks like an initial has been rubbed out. It may be nothing, but see what you think. Get a document expert to look at it if you think it's necessary."

He took it with a grimace. Indicating the tidy piles of paper on his desk, he said, "I'm overwhelmed. It's starting to look like yours."

"Never. Takes years of practice."

"Vail came through with a client list," he said, "although he says it might be incomplete. There's no record of Noelle Winthall being a patient. Also, I recognized the names of a few celebrities and wouldn't be surprised if they're packing death right now, wondering if some gossip column's going to spill the beans."

"According to your friend, Gilda Milton, Halstead claimed to be offering a unique cloning service for lesbians and gays. She said that Halstead stressed that this was outside the law, so the whole thing had to be totally confidential. She thinks he had some takers but claims she doesn't know who they are. I imagine they'll turn up on the client list but cloning won't be mentioned."

"Rather ambitious of him," said Bourke. "Based on what Joan Yaller says about the stage human cloning's at, I doubt the good doctor could deliver on his promises."

"Exactly. And that might make someone very angry."

"It's a reasonable motive for murder," said Bourke. "People get very emotional about pregnancies and babies."

He and Pat were going through exactly that emotional time, thought Carol, so some of the issues in the case must be uncomfortably close to home for him.

Handing him her notebook, she said, "Elaine Kaynes is the whistle-blower, according to Gilda, and that's been confirmed by Madeline. These are the names of the people *The Shipley Report* has got to back up the claims that cloning's going on in the clinic."

"Okay, I'll line up Ms. Kaynes as soon as possible."

"Madeline says she'll be in the studios this afternoon, recording a segment for the show. I said we'd be there at four. In the meantime, get as much background on her as possible."

As Carol turned to go, he added, "You've got a visitor. Leta Halstead turned up unannounced about fifteen minutes ago. I had her identify her husband's personal effects — the ring, wallet, keys — and she said they were definitely his, but she didn't seem very interested in getting them back. Now she's sitting in your office talking with Anne. I offered to call you, but she said she only had a few moments before a luncheon date, although she's still here."

Anne and Leta Halstead were chatting like old friends when Carol opened the door of her office. Leta immediately rose to her feet. Wearing a short pink dress and high-heeled pink sandals, she looked anything but a new widow. "Inspector Ashton," she said in her light, clear voice, "I probably should have called, but I did want to see you as soon as possible."

"You've come to make an official statement?"

For a moment she looked confused. "A statement? No, I've come to talk to you about who might have killed Brin."

Carol gestured for Anne to stay. "Please sit down," she said to Leta.

Sinking into her own comfortable swivel chair, Carol said, "Do you suspect somebody?"

"Frankly, I imagine there are a lot of people who aren't sorry Brin's dead."

"Can I have some names?" As she spoke, Carol looked over at Anne, who already had a pen and a notepad ready.

Leta took a deep breath, and the words spilled out. "There's Gilda Milton. Brin never believed me when I told him, but I've sensed it for a long time. He trusted her, but Gilda hated him, resented him. And Ursula Vail — she's a poisonous creature. She'd do anything, say anything, to advance her husband. She knew Brin was going to dump him, break up the partnership." She made a scornful noise. "Partnership? Bill Vail doesn't pull his weight, and never has."

"You believe these people had motives to kill your husband?"

Leta frowned at Carol's mild inquiry. "That's what I'm telling you, Inspector."

"Do you have any firm evidence? Threats you or somebody else might have heard? Anything in writing?"

"That's your job, I believe." She leaned to collect her pink leather bag from under her chair. "I have to go."

She paused in the middle of the office. The harsh fluorescent light reflected on her glossy dark hair. She was, Carol decided, very attractive, and possibly unbalanced.

"I don't know who else to say this to, but I thought . . ." She trailed off, biting her lip.

"Yes?" Carol gave her an encouraging look. "What is it?"

"I suppose you'll think this is awful, that I could even say it, but my parents — Brin disappointed them, the way he disappointed me."

"You think your parents might have wished your husband harm?"

Leta gave Carol a tiny, unhappy smile. "Did you notice? All those women around Brin having babies, and not me? And I'm to have a brother, did you hear? At least, that's what Brin said, but then, it didn't work out."

Leta looked at Carol, then at Anne. "I've said too much."

Carol tried, but Leta Halstead turned away her questions. "Please," she said, clutching her pink bag with both hands, "I must go."

Anne saw her out, then came back to say to Carol, "Wow!"

"Yes," said Carol. "It's difficult to know what to believe. See if you can find out her medical history."

"Right," said Anne, "and I'm betting you one of Maureen's pineapple doughnuts that there's at least one psychiatrist in the mix."

CHAPTER EIGHT

"This is Noelle Winthall," said the confident voice on the phone. "I imagine you'll be trying to find me any moment now, so I'm short-circuiting the process."

Carol immediately recognized the journalist's fast-paced, assured voice. "You had an appointment to see Dr. Halstead on Wednesday," Carol said.

"And since he's been dispatched to heaven or hell, whichever he deserves," said the journalist, "I was sure you'd want to talk with me."

In her mind's eye Carol could see Noelle's lop-

81

sided, disarming grin. She asked, "Do you have an opinion regarding which it will be?"

"I wouldn't hazard a guess, Inspector, but I'm sorry he's dead for selfish reasons."

"A good doctor is hard to find?"

Noelle laughed at Carol's dry tone. "Not exactly. I wonder if we could meet? I'd be delighted to buy you a coffee, a meal, whatever. I'll be claiming it as a business expense, so it'll be my treat."

Carol was wary, having been taught the hard way that many journalists should be treated with caution. Noelle could be wired and have a photographer standing by for a candid shot of a police officer getting friendly with a reporter. Carol didn't consider herself paranoid, as on several occasions her misgivings had been well founded, and she had no intention of providing fodder for an article on the Halstead murder or anything else.

She said, "Perhaps we can cover the main questions now, on the phone."

"No way, my dear Inspector! I need to see you alone, face-to-face. Then I'll tell you everything I know. I'm going to have to trust you to keep as much as you can private."

The sincerity in her voice, plus the fact that Carol had found her dependable in the past, convinced Carol it was worth the risk. She looked at her watch. "I have to be out of here just after three for an appointment. That doesn't leave much time."

"Let's make it coffee, then." Noelle named a coffee shop a ten-minute walk from the Police Centre. "I'll see you there in a quarter of an hour. Okay?"

Before leaving, Carol told Bourke about the meeting. "Gilda Milton thought she was one of

Halstead's patients," she said, "but I think she may have been there as a journalist."

"I'll pick you up at the coffee shop just after three," said Bourke, adding with a grin, "That is, if I can get past the media crush."

Carol enjoyed being outside walking in the warm air rather than sitting in a car. She held her face up to the sun as she strode along, squinting through her sunglasses at the brazen summer glare. It was good to be alive, to be healthy.

And happy? Two out of three wasn't bad. She mentally mocked herself. Happiness was a state of mind, and she had everything to attain it. Contentment, though. That was another matter.

Noelle Winthall was sitting at a tiny table at the back of the room away from the door. The seductive odor of ground coffee and hot milk pleased Carol, as did the baroque lines of the machine hissing on the counter. The coffee shop was half full, and Carol automatically checked out the other customers. Some were in animated conversation. Others sat reading or staring into space. She didn't recognize anyone, and no one seemed to be concealing a press camera.

"Hi," said Noelle, getting to her feet. "Thank you for coming."

She was more heavily tanned than Carol remembered, her skin prematurely aged. Although Carol estimated she would only be in her mid-thirties, deep crow's-feet radiated from the corners of her eyes when she smiled. She looked fit. Her stomach was flat in tight jeans, and her arms in her sleeveless top were lightly muscled and firm.

Carol slid onto the spindly wooden chair opposite her. "I'm afraid we only have a few minutes."

"I'll talk fast." She signaled for attention, and they ordered coffee. Carol had her usual black, unadorned caffeine fix; Noelle had an elaborate iced concoction in a tall glass.

Using a long-handled spoon to play with the cap of frothy cream that topped her drink, Noelle said, "I know you're gay."

"It's not a secret."

"It was, for a long time."

"Look," said Carol, feeling impatience rising, "either we talk about the Halstead case or I'm out of here."

She took a gulp of her coffee and scalded her tongue. Coming here had obviously been a mistake. The journalist was fishing for material, probably something like "Gays in the Police Service."

"I *am* talking about the Halstead case." Noelle dropped her voice. "My partner and I — her name's Beth, by the way — went to the clinic because we heard on the grapevine that Brin Halstead was offering something extraordinary. Something we could use."

Putting down her cup, Carol said, "I presume you wanted a baby together. There's nothing extraordinary about that."

Noelle looked around, as if anxious that no one should overhear. "We didn't want men involved in any way." She half smiled. "That's ambiguous. What I mean is, we didn't want to use sperm. Do you know what I mean?"

"Cloning?" Carol kept the incredulity out of her voice. To her, this was still the stuff of science fiction.

"So you've heard the rumors. Well, it's true. Brin

Halstead said he'd achieved viable babies several times. Beth was keen, but I was doubtful. I've got a reasonable science background, and so he showed me everything. I was convinced. We went ahead with it."

Catching Carol's quizzical look, she added, "No, not me. It cost a lot, almost everything we've got, but Beth's carrying two babies. One's my clone. One's hers. They'll be born next March."

It was hard to remember when she had been rendered speechless, but Carol realized this was one of those times. She stared at Noelle, aware that the ramifications of what she'd been told were tremendous. Then cool common sense reasserted itself. It was much more likely to be a con game on Halstead's part than a true reproductive breakthrough.

"And it's not just us," said Noelle. "There are gay guys who want to have children that will be totally theirs and no one else's. Men have to use a surrogate mother, of course, but the baby is the clone of one of them, or both, if they choose to do what we have. Can you imagine that?"

"With difficulty," said Carol, shaking her head.

"There's more," Noelle said in a low voice, leaning over the table until their heads were almost touching. "I'm writing a book about it all. There's no way it isn't going to be one of the most sensational true-life stories ever."

"Did Halstead know about this?"

"Know?" said Noelle. "He was all for it. We were negotiating a contract between us where he agreed to supply all the technical details in return for half the royalties. Beth's terribly worried that her name will get out, partly because her family are the typical religious bigots, but mainly because she thinks we'll be hounded to death by the loonies on the right, so I'm going to use pseudonyms."

Carol said, "I don't imagine Dr. Halstead would have liked his real name used, either. Cloning is against the law."

"So arrest me." Noelle was scornful. "The kids couldn't be more ours. Hell — they *are* us!"

She grabbed her glass and took a long swallow. Wiping the cream mustache from her upper lip, she said, "Brin Halstead was after all the publicity he could get, so he wanted to use his real name. He told me he was sure that cloning would be treated like any other advance in science, where the initial incomprehension and knee-jerk legislation would be followed by acceptance, once the techniques became established and everyone can see the advantages."

Carol checked her watch. Bourke would be outside any minute. "Can you throw any light on Halstead's death?"

"Maybe I can. Our appointment on Wednesday afternoon was to discuss the contract and settle all the small details. He was twitchy, upset. He wanted to know when I could get a book proposal in the marketplace, not here in Australia, but straight to America where the big money is. Said he had to have a substantial advance as soon as possible, and he got angry when I said it couldn't happen overnight. When I left he was white and sweating."

"You thought he was afraid of something or someone?"

Noelle flipped her hand. "I thought he was terrified for his life," she said.

* * * * *

To call Madeline's room an office was not to do it justice. It was really a luxurious suite, in vast contrast to the utilitarian exterior of the television station. It was very little altered from the first time that Carol had seen it. The theme of beige and blue remained, and the deep pile carpet was still thick enough to imagine one could sink into it ankle deep.

One wall looked out into a courtyard, reminding Carol of the Halstead Clinic, though it was more elegant here. In the center a small fountain played, surrounded by low stone benches, and the greenery was strictly disciplined in terra-cotta pots.

Nor had Madeline changed much since Carol's initial meeting with her. She wore her copper hair shorter, and perhaps the expression lines on her face were a little deeper, but otherwise she was the same almost too beautiful television personality whose wide gray eyes and easy smile could beguile the toughest interviewee.

"You owe me, you two," said Madeline to Carol and Bourke. "I've made this very easy for you. Co-operated with the police" — she looked impossibly virtuous — "and delivered a witness to you with my very own hands."

Bourke laughed. "Sure," he said. "We were just stumbling around in the dark until you put on the light."

As Madeline chuckled along with him, Carol reflected that Madeline had always liked Bourke, although the feeling was not always reciprocated.

There was a knock at the door, and one of

Madeline's staff ushered in an angular, awkward woman. Carol surveyed the head of the Halstead Clinic's nursing staff. She had good bones in her face, and the television makeup had accentuated her large, pale blue eyes. She looked to be in her mid-forties.

"Have we finished?" she said to Madeline, her manner a combination of deference and pride.

Madeline was gracious. "Elaine, you've done a wonderful job. I'll be talking with my people to see if we need you for anything else. In the meantime, I've arranged for some refreshments."

"Oh, good. I would like something." The woman flicked her glance around the room. "This is very nice."

Madeline indicated Carol and Bourke. "And I'd like to introduce you to Detective Inspector Carol Ashton and Detective Sergeant Mark Bourke."

Hiding a grin at the way Madeline rolled the titles off her tongue, Carol shook hands with Elaine Kaynes. She had a dry, slack grip, and she avoided Carol's eyes.

Madeline supervised the placing of a tray containing coffee and tea on a table in the center of an arrangement of deep blue lounge chairs.

"I'll leave you then," she said, with a meaningful look at Carol, "but I do hope to see you and Mark before you go."

Carol indicated one of the blue chairs, and, after a moment's hesitation, Elaine Kaynes seated herself.

"Everyone's so nice here," she said. "They've all been so thoughtful. Nothing's been too much trouble. I've even had a chauffeured car to pick me up and take me home."

Carol had the tart thought that, for television

programs like Madeline's, keeping people like Elaine
Kaynes as happy as possible was a pragmatic move
designed to keep a source talking.

"So you've enjoyed the experience?" Carol said,
intending to put the woman at her ease.

"I have. And Madeline's been so very, very kind."

She leaned forward and took a dainty triangular
sandwich. "I know, Inspector, that you're *very* familiar
with television. I've seen you on it so many times,
and you're really quite excellent, almost professional."

Carol saw Bourke's lips twitch.

Elaine examined the little sandwich carefully, then
bit it in half and swallowed. She said, "It's just so
dreadful about Dr. Halstead."

"You saw him yesterday?"

"Oh, no. I've been taking a few days leave." She
gestured with the remaining half of the sandwich. "I
needed time off to come here, to the television
station."

"So when did you see him last?"

Elaine popped the sandwich into her mouth and
chewed as she considered. "That would be on
Monday, late afternoon, but I did *speak* with him on
Wednesday morning. It was just about scheduling a
procedure for a patient. Nothing important."

Bourke said, "Did Dr. Halstead have any idea that
you had gone to the media about the clinic?"

"No, no idea at all. Of course, I was prepared to
resign before the program aired, but I wonder now if
I need to, since it was really nothing to do with Dr.
Vail, and he'll now be in charge of the clinic, I
imagine."

"And you get on well with Dr. Vail?"

She gave Bourke a suspicious glance, as though

there might be more to the question than it appeared, but his serious, homely face obviously reassured her. "Dr. Vail is very particular, but I like that. Unfortunately he doesn't have the *vision* that Dr. Halstead had."

She leaned forward and picked up a cup. "Tea, anyone? Coffee?"

When both Bourke and Carol indicated they would pass on refreshments, Elaine Kaynes said, "Well, if you'll excuse me, I'll help myself."

She made quite a business of pouring tea, stirring in sugar, and selecting a second little sandwich and an iced cupcake to put on her plate. Then she settled back with the air of one ready to face questioning.

Carol said, "Why did you feel you had to go to the media?"

"Not the *media,* Inspector Ashton, *The Shipley Report.* I consider that it's head and shoulders above other programs of its type."

Bourke said, using a harder tone than he had previously, "You've making some very serious accusations about Dr. Halstead."

"I've told what I've seen, and I'm not proud to say that I waited far too long to come forward. When I first had suspicions that things were wrong, I should have spoken up. But I needed my job — I have an invalid husband, you know — and I couldn't, at first, believe that Dr. Halstead would do such things."

"Please be more explicit," said Bourke. There was an edge of impatience in his voice. "I don't have to remind you this is a murder case."

A flicker of consternation, perhaps fear, crossed

her face. Her cup clattered against the saucer as she put it down. Carol thought that the nurse had enjoyed being the center of attention so far, but that the reality of the situation was beginning to dawn on her.

"It *was* murder?"

"Someone beat his head in and set the laboratory on fire," said Carol, deliberately brutal.

This time the woman's face showed unmistakable distress. "That's dreadful. And perhaps I'm to blame..."

"In what way?"

She didn't seem to hear Bourke's question. "If only I'd kept quiet, but I couldn't. What was happening at the clinic was wrong, and someone had to do something about it."

"Cloning?" said Bourke.

"Yes, everyone's interested in *that*," she said with some scorn. "Even the people here at the station wanted to concentrate on cloning and its sensational side. Personally, I see nothing wrong with it. Soon cloning will be accepted the way IVF is now. I totally support everything Dr. Halstead was doing in the area. It's what is going to propel the Halstead Clinic to the forefront of genetic research."

"If it wasn't cloning, what was it?"

Elaine Kaynes looked down, as if embarrassed. "What I couldn't accept, what I had to speak out about, was something else entirely. Dr. Halstead was using his own sperm to fertilize eggs. He was telling patients that the sperm belonged to screened donors, but much of the time it was *his*."

A spasm of amusement twisted her mouth. "Can

you imagine? All those proud parents, all those sons and daughters of Dr. Halstead's out there — and not one of them knowing it?"

Carol had evaded Madeline's invitation to dinner and Bourke's offer to take potluck with him and Pat, and had escaped to the soothing silence of her house, so she swore under her breath when the phone began to ring.

"I know you're busy on a case," said Aunt Sarah, "but I'm ringing to check on you. Are you eating properly?"

As her closest living relative, her aunt took her position seriously. Carol looked at the frozen dinner she was about to shove into the microwave, and said, "I'm fine. Eating a very balanced diet."

"And how's Sybil?"

Carol ran her bare foot down Sinker's back, and was rewarded with a purr. "She's fine, too."

An exasperated sigh came down the line from a hundred kilometers away in the Blue Mountains. "You know what I mean. She isn't there with you, is she?"

"If you're asking, are we still living apart, the answer's yes."

"What are you going to do, Carol?"

"About Sybil? Aunt Sarah, she won't even come into the house."

"Would *you*?"

Carol found herself gesturing to empty air, as though Aunt Sarah could see her and be convinced.

"I said I'd change it. I said I'd gut the building if it made a difference. Rebuild it so it is nothing like it was before."

"You could live at her place. You like the beach."

"This is my *home!*" Carol looked around the kitchen, then out through the double sliding doors into the darkness, where trees crowded up to the wide wooden veranda. She belonged here, loved everything about it. It had been her parents' home, and now it was hers.

Aunt Sarah said, "I wonder if you really understand. Sybil had the most dreadful experience in your house. I've talked to her about it. She nearly died."

"I know. I was there."

"But *you* weren't the victim, Carol."

"But I do understand."

"No you don't, Carol. You see horrors every day, and you're hardened to them. Sybil isn't."

"Hell . . ."

"I know you love that house, but you're going to have to decide."

"In time, Sybil will be okay. The feeling will fade, I'm sure it will."

"And if it isn't okay?"

"I don't know, Aunt Sarah. I'll cross that bridge when I come to it."

"I think you've come to the bridge already, my dear. You just don't want to admit it."

"Aunt Sarah, did I tell you about David's performance at his school sports day?"

"I may be old, but I can sense a change in the subject." Her tone was dry.

Carol smiled. She could visualize Aunt Sarah's

tanned face, her warm eyes, her halo of irrepressible white hair. "I'm going to talk to Sybil this weekend. Maybe we can work something out."

"Maybe," said Aunt Sarah. She didn't sound convinced.

CHAPTER NINE

The run through the bush was soothing, with Olga loping at her side and periodically dashing off to hunt down some intriguing smell. On Saturday mornings Carol got up a little later, so the early cool of the day had gone, and soon Carol's T-shirt was clinging wetly to her skin. She raised a hand to acknowledge a runner going the other way on the narrow dirt path. He gave her a head-to-toe glance of appreciation, and she smiled to herself, wondering what he would think if he knew she had a little

Glock automatic in the small of her back, held snugly by a holster in the waistband of her shorts.

Once she would never have dreamed of taking a weapon with her while she ran. Now her attitude was tempered by experiences that had made her precaution in arming herself at all times seem sensible foresight.

Now that it was hot, the birds had fallen silent. All that Carol could hear was the rhythmic pound of her feet, her own breathing, and Olga's panting. She thought that the smell of the bush, that wonderful combination of subtle scents overlaid by the eucalyptus of the gum trees, must be unique to Australia.

Here, on this rough path, she could be a thousand miles away from Sydney's vibrant life, from murder and lies, yet if she looked to her left, over the waters of Middle Harbour to the other shore, the illusion would be broken.

Carol turned for home with reluctance, the questions of the Halstead case flooding into her mind. Where had Brin Halstead been from eight o'clock, when his wife saw him last, until his murder? Jeff Duke had called to say that examination of the stomach contents indicated that the food had been digested for at least an hour, but beyond that he wouldn't even make an educated guess at time of death.

Duke had added with a snort of laughter, "And the dental records match, so you can kiss good-bye to any idea that Halstead's enjoying life in Brazil."

Why was Halstead in such financial trouble? Maureen Oatland was investigating the possibility of gambling or drugs, but Carol felt it was more likely that the doctor had been paying someone off.

Her thoughts went to Leta Halstead's parents. Iniga and Perry Alaric had every reason to be happy with their son-in-law, presuming that what Iniga had said about a surrogate carrying a child to replace their dead son was true. Iniga Alaric had been so positive that it *was* a son that Carol made a mental note to find out whether gender selection was one of the services offered by the Halstead Clinic.

As she jogged out of the bush onto a street leading to her home, she called Olga to heel. She mentally checked through her schedule for the day as she slackened to a slow jog and then a fast walk.

At ten she would meet Mark Bourke in Leichhardt to interview Cindy Farr, one of the clinic's surrogate mothers, and her brother, Howard Farr, who had threatened to bash in Brin Halstead's head. Bourke had turned up a record of minor arrests for Howard Stephen Farr, commonly known as Howie, but there had been nothing serious, mainly alter-cations where punches had been thrown.

At two Dr. Vail had insisted that Bourke meet him at the clinic to discuss "important new matters," so Carol had taken the opportunity to make an appointment to speak with Ursula Vail alone, believing that she would get more out of her if her husband wasn't present. Bourke had checked with a document expert, and the consensus was that the erased entry for seven o'clock on the day Halstead died was definitely the letter *U*, so Carol was interested to hear where Ursula claimed to have been at that time.

Carol was determined to squeeze David into the schedule somewhere. She'd told him she'd call him this morning to say when she'd pick him up, and he'd said "Oh yeah, sure" with such exaggerated weariness that Carol felt a stab of remorse, mixed with irritation. Like cats, children could wring the very last atom of guilt out of any situation.

She'd set aside the evening for Sybil. She wanted to arrive early at Sybil's house so that they'd have time for a walk along the beach before dinner. Carol allowed herself a thrill of anticipation. It was going to be a good evening.

She put a happy, panting Olga through the gate of her neighbor's house and went to shower and change. Before entering the house, she walked slowly around it, eyeing its familiar lines, allowing its memories to wash over her.

She'd lived here all her life, until she went to university and shared a flat with friends. Then she'd married Justin Hart and moved to a grandiose house on one of the best streets in the most exclusive area of the Eastern Suburbs.

Her marriage shattered, her parents dead within months of each other, Carol had come back to this house to heal. She paused by the window that had once been her bedroom, half smiling as she remembered her ten-year-old self scrambling out at two in the morning. A friend had dared her that she wouldn't move a garish pink plastic flamingo from the ornamental fishpond in one neighbor's garden and position it in front of the posh place up the street.

She turned to go inside, her smile fading as she

thought of David and of how many things she hadn't shared of his growing up. Now he was a teenager, and he seemed more a stranger than her son.

Dressed soberly in a cobalt blue tailored dress, Carol joined the Saturday morning shoppers, many of whom seemed to drive without purpose or direction. Stuck in a mini traffic jam, caused by a minor collision between two such drivers at the Seaforth shops, Carol flicked on the radio to fill the time.

"And now, after an important message, a breaking story . . ."

Automatically tuning out the commercial, she had the idle thought that it was odd to describe stories as breaking. Were they breaking like waves? Or perhaps tight little facts packed together were splitting apart . . .

". . . Sydney, this A.M. Dr. Brin Halstead, murdered fertility specialist, whose charred body was found in the ruins of his prestigious Halstead Clinic earlier this week, has been accused of serious IVF irregularities. As yet unsubstantiated reports detail a shocking situation, where sperm bank specimens chosen by patients using the IVF system were not used, the specimen being replaced by sperm from Dr. Halstead himself. And there are suggestions of even more outrageous practices. Stay tuned for further developments in this heartbreaking story . . ."

Madeline would be furious, Carol was sure. *The Shipley Report* had a very tight security on forthcoming exposés, and anyone who was a major source of information was required to sign a confidentiality agreement.

The cars ahead of her began to move. Edging past the still-arguing drivers of the damaged vehicles, she thought what an advantage it was for the media that Dr. Halstead was no longer alive. One could not defame the dead, so there were no longer tight restrictions on what could be said. Had he been living, a great deal of infering and skirting around the truth would have occurred. Now, she thought, accelerating toward Spit Bridge, for journalists it was full speed ahead.

In spite of the traffic, Carol arrived at Cindy Farr's house in Leichhardt five minutes early. Bourke, who was rarely late for anything, was already there. When Carol parked behind him, he got out of his car.

"Got some info for you, Carol. That door-to-door of the area wasn't a total waste of time, after all. We've got a witness who saw something going on near the Halstead Clinic about when the fire started. I had a quick word with him, and Anne's getting a statement. In essence all you need to know is that this guy lives a couple of streets away and that he was walking his dog near the clinic when he saw someone drive around the block about three or four times. Said he noticed because his dog's an old bloke, so he takes forever to sniff and lift his leg to mark his territory, which meant they were hanging around the clinic area for a while."

"Could he identify the vehicle?"

"No, just a light colored car. He thought a recent model, probably expensive, but he wasn't sure." Bourke grinned. "He isn't into cars. Would you believe, he rides a bicycle to work? He only realized it was the same one about the third time around. The interesting thing is, he had the impression it was a woman driving. No idea of age or hair color, but he said he knew the driver was female."

"What time was this?"

"He says he takes his dog out a bit after nine on pretty much the same route every time. It takes twenty minutes to half an hour to get to the street the clinic's on, so that makes it roughly nine-thirty. Seems to work out — the guy hadn't been home for long when he heard the fire engines screaming along Oxford Street, and they logged in with an arrival at the clinic of ten-eighteen."

Carol said, without expecting a positive answer, "He didn't see a stray vehicle in the parking lot, did he?"

"He didn't notice any," said Bourke. "But then again, if you were going to torch a place, wouldn't you leave your vehicle in the street at least some distance away?"

"Not if I were lugging a jerry can of petrol," said Carol. "I'd be inclined to go to the back entrance." She frowned. "Or maybe I'd leave the can concealed close to the building, and park somewhere else. It wouldn't be too far away, because I'd want to make a quick exit."

"Of course," said Bourke, "we could be looking at this the wrong way. What if Brin Halstead had the jerry can in the boot of his BMW parked in the loading dock? Maybe he was going to burn the building himself so he could collect the insurance, and someone caught him at it and objected."

"Some objection," said Carol. "This person bashes

Halstead to death and then sets the fire he objected to?"

Bourke feigned offense at her mockery. "Naturally I have a scenario to cover that," he said. "Our perp doesn't mean to kill Halstead, but he gets carried away. He looks at the body, the petrol's already there, so what would be more natural than covering up his tracks by starting a fire?"

Noticing a curtain twitching in the front window, she said, "We're being watched. Perhaps we'd better go in."

Cindy Farr and her brother lived in a little house that had almost certainly been built as a workman's cottage a hundred years or so before. The purity of its practical lines had been blurred by neglect and the addition of such extras as a hideous canopy of corrugated green Fiberglas positioned over the front door.

"Nice decorative touch," said Bourke, grinning at Carol's look of distaste. "And I bet the inside's crash hot, too."

The young woman who opened the door to Bourke's knock was a bottle blond with a hard expression and a discontented mouth. "You the cops? You've been standing outside long enough. Better come in, but don't expect to get anything out of me. I don't know nothing."

She turned on her heel, moving with incongruous grace for one so heavily pregnant, and disappeared down a short hall and into a room. Bourke raised his eyebrows to Carol and closed the front door.

Years of wear and dirt tramped in had reduced the hall's carpet runner into a thin, gray-brown strip.

The cream background and flower design of the wallpaper was smeared with oily marks. Carol felt herself recoiling, not wanting even her clothing to brush against the fabric of the house.

Her aversion was heightened when she and Bourke entered the sitting room into which Cindy Farr had disappeared. The red vinyl of the settee and two matching chairs was grimy, particularly on the arms, where greasy hands had left an accumulation of dark smudges. No one had bothered to clear away dinner dishes from the night before, and newspapers and magazines had been dropped casually on tables and on the floor. Images danced across the screen of a large television set, but the sound was muted to a faint grumble of noise.

"This is me brother, Howie."

The man Cindy indicated was whippet thin, but looked formidable. He wore faded jeans and a grubby T-shirt, and his arms showed hard muscle. Slumped in one of the grimy chairs, he held a can of beer in one dangling hand and a lighted cigarette in the other. He didn't bother to speak or get up, but simply gave them a flat, reptilian stare, then switched his attention back to the television.

"You better sit." Cindy cleared a pile of magazines from the red settee, and as she sank gingerly onto the stained vinyl, Carol noticed with astonishment that the top magazine was the latest *Scientific American*.

Bourke smoothly introduced himself and Carol and thanked the two of them for being available on a Saturday morning.

"Didn't have no choice, did we?" said Cindy.

Howie grunted, apparently in agreement, and took a swallow of beer from his can, but his gaze didn't leave the screen.

Bourke opened his notebook. Carol said, "How long have you been a surrogate mother for clients of the Halstead Clinic?"

"A while. Had two healthy kids for them, right to full term, but lost a few too. They don't always take, you know. I'd say about five years." She lowered herself into the vinyl chair next to her brother. "Put that fag out, Howie," she commanded. "I can't have secondhand smoke when I'm carrying."

Without change of expression, he leaned over to stub his cigarette out in a battered metal ashtray overflowing with butts.

Cindy went on, "It's just a job to me. Where else could I make money this good doing nothing much at all?"

"On your bloody back," mumbled Howie.

"Oh, *you*!" Cindy said, punching her brother's arm. Howie smiled slightly, but his attention never shifted from the television.

Bourke said conversationally, "You like children?"

She gave him a look of incredulity. "Can't hack 'em, specially babies. Noisy little brutes who scream half the time, when they're not dirtying their nappies or throwing up. The nine months is okay, I'm well paid for it, but then you're on your own. I'm not into breast feeding, whatever the do-gooders say. I'm willing to express a bit of milk to start it off — after that, it's good-bye. I always say to them, you don't like it, find someone else."

"Do you know any of the other surrogate mothers?" asked Bourke.

"Yeah. A couple." She looked at her brother. "We know bloody Faye, don't we, Howie?" When he didn't respond, she repeated, "Bloody Faye," in a reflective tone.

"Why bloody Faye?" asked Carol, suppressing the impulse to smile.

Cindy pursed her lips over the question. "I 'spose it's not her fault, but *I* don't get the plush jobs — no, it's bloody Faye. I mean, *she's* the one the bloody Alarics are carrying on about. Like, would you believe, they set her and her mum up in this house, and gave her a *car*." She shook her head. "Jesus! I should be so lucky."

"This would be Faye Pickerson?" said Bourke.

"Yeah." Cindy grinned, and Carol noticed she had excellent teeth. "Least, that's the name she's using at the moment."

"And Faye's the surrogate mother for Iniga and Perry Alaric?"

She gave Bourke a long-suffering look. "That's what I said, didn't I? Mind, if I were him, I'd be asking for paternity testing."

"You mean the child's not his?"

"It's a fetus, not a child," said Cindy, correcting him. "And I'm not saying no more. I just heard a few things, and could be they mean nothing."

With a cheeky grin, she added, "Good thing this isn't the U.K., eh? There a guy can post off samples of his saliva and his kid's, plus money, to this company, see, and find out a few weeks later if he's the dad." Her face alive with amusement, she went on, "And you know, about one out of five times, he isn't!"

Carol said, "When did you last see Dr. Halstead?

The question wiped all amusement from Cindy's face. "Not for ages," she said. "Had no reason to, once I was preggers. The clients pick the doctor and pay all the medical stuff. Halstead gets reports, but I don't have to see him. He rings me now and then to see if everything's okay. It always is, 'cause I look after myself, okay?"

"So when did Dr. Halstead last call you?"

Cindy frowned at Carol's persistence. "Jeez, I dunno. Week before last, maybe. Like, I don't write it down."

"So everything was going smoothly?"

Suspicious, she said, "Yeah . . ."

"Then why," said Bourke, "was your brother in Dr. Halstead's office last week, threatening him with bodily harm?"

Howie dragged his gaze from the television. "It's a lie. Who told you that?" He slapped his beer can down on the side table by his chair. "I'll straighten them out."

"You won't straighten anyone out," said Carol, her voice hard. "Brin Halstead's been murdered, and a few days before he died, a witness says that you promised to beat his head in. That makes you a prime suspect."

"The hell it does! I was just trying to frighten the bastard."

"Why?"

Howie jerked his head in Cindy's direction. "Cin, here, she gets the rough end of the stick. Doesn't get treated proper. Doesn't get as much money as others. I went in to put it right, but fucking Halstead tried to put it over on me, talk his way out of it. I just wanted to scare the shit out of him, but I wasn't going to *do* anything." He glared at them. "And I didn't."

The red vinyl squeaked as he shifted in his chair. "Look, if I did him in, do you think I'd still be sitting around here? I'd be long gone."

"Where were you on Wednesday evening?" Carol asked.

"When the bugger was killed? I had a few drinks with the boys, and got home here, about —" He broke off to glance in his sister's direction. "Whatcha say, Cin? About eight?"

"About eight," she agreed. Together they looked at Carol and Bourke.

"Convenient," said Bourke. "A double alibi."

"Watch it," said Howie, thrusting out a belligerent chin. "You're not going to hang this on Cin or me. Why don't you pick on that queer at the clinic? He's the one that dobbed me in, isn't he? Well, think about this. It's his boyfriend's brat that Cin's carrying, and little Tommy isn't too happy about the whole deal, I can tell you that."

Further questions on this topic got nowhere, so Carol said, "Ms. Farr —"

"Jesus. Call me Cin, everybody does."

Carol, avoiding any name at all, went on, "Does the Halstead Clinic offer gender preselection?"

"Too right. I can tell you all about it." Cindy caught Bourke's dubious expression, and her face reddened. "Think I'm stupid since I just have babies, do you?"

Bourke grew a little pink himself. "Of course not."

Cindy, her chin high, turned back to Carol. "What you have to do is to up the odds on whether it'll be a boy or a girl. See, it's the sperm that determines the sex of the baby."

She cast Bourke a cool look, then continued, "An X sperm linking up with an egg makes a girl, and a Y sperm makes a boy."

Howie's mouth twitched. "Up the Ys!" he said, his gaze back on the television set.

"Shut up," she said without animosity. He gave no sign that he had heard her.

"Anyway," Cindy went on, "what you need to do is get the sperm into two little bunches, one male and the other female. Halstead did it using a protein solution that separated X from Y. Then all you need is IVF and you've got the son or daughter that you want."

"How reliable is it?" asked Carol, interested.

"Pretty good. Works about seventy-five percent of the time." She sent Bourke a challenging look. "I 'spose you'd always go for sons, wouldn't you."

"I wouldn't care."

"Oh, yeah." It was obvious she didn't believe him.

"We may have more questions in the future," said Carol, preparing to leave. Cindy rolled her eyes. Howie grunted.

Outside the house, Bourke said to Carol, "What do you think?"

"I think we should pay an unscheduled visit to Thomas Lorant and partner later today. Have you got his address?"

Bourke went to his car and came back with a leather folder. Locating the list of clinic staff, he said, "Lorant lives quite near the clinic. He could walk to work, if he was feeling energetic."

"Okay, I'm just about to call David and tell him

I'm picking him up for lunch in a few minutes. Then I'm seeing Ursula Vail at the same time you're meeting her husband at the clinic. When you finish with Vail, call me on the mobile phone. We can meet at Lorant's place. If he isn't there, we haven't lost anything. If he is, it could be interesting."

"And Faye Pickerson?" He checked the folder. "She lives in West Ryde. Do you want me to line something up for tomorrow?"

"Try the afternoon," Carol said, thinking that she wanted to keep Sunday morning for coffee and croissants with Sybil.

"Can't get over it," said Bourke as he closed the folder. "These women having other people's babies." He made a face. "They call it *rent-a-womb*," he said.

Carol looked at his disapproving expression, wondering whether, should it really ever come down to it, Pat and Bourke would consider a surrogate.

As if he had read her mind, Bourke said with a rueful smile, "Hey, who am I to judge? If it were the only way . . ." He shrugged. "But not cloning. I don't agree with that."

"Aren't identical twins clones?" said Carol. "They share the same DNA."

He looked nonplussed. "I'd never thought of that. I suppose, in some way they are clones." He laughed. "Don't give me these ethical challenges, Carol. I'm just not up to them!"

CHAPTER TEN

David opened the front door. "Hello, Mum."

She saw herself reflected in his blond hair and green eyes. Kissing his cheek, she thought how tall he was becoming. "What do you want to do, darling?"

He eyed her warily. "How long have we got?"

"Ages. Well . . . a couple of hours."

"That's not long enough to see a movie or *anything.*"

"I'm sorry, but I'm on a case."

He kicked his foot against the doorjamb. "You always are."

Carol tried to sound reasonable. "It's my job, David. I don't work nine-to-five hours."

He seemed to cheer up at this. "Okay."

It was her turn to be wary. "What would you like to do?" she said, bracing herself for his reply. If it was something she didn't have time for, they were unlikely to part on good terms.

"I'd like to see where you work. Then we can have a pizza."

Surprised, Carol said, "Why do you want to see where I work? It isn't very exciting — just a building and an office."

He thrust out his bottom lip. "That's what I want to do, but if you don't . . ."

"Of course we can go there, if you want to, but —"

"Eleanor," he shouted, cutting Carol off. "Mum's here. I'll get something to eat while we're out. Back soon."

He bounded down the steps and scrambled into her car. Carol followed, wryly amused at David's single-minded pursuit of what he wanted. It was a characteristic, she had to admit, that she had herself.

As she drove, he chattered unselfconsciously, seeming younger than the solemn young man who had met her at the door. He told her about his running, and Carol said at school she'd been a good runner, too.

"Oh, yeah, Mum, sure. I mean, I know you *jog,* but that's not sprinting."

She chuckled at his derision and made a bet that she could beat him over a kilometer.

"No way!" he hooted.

As she parked the car and he hopped out, laughing, Carol wished that it could always be like this. And why couldn't it? She would be ruthless and make more time for him in her life. He loved Sybil — she would ask him to stay over down at the beach.

When he was younger, Carol had explained to David her relationship with Sybil. In general terms, she thought. In very general terms. She was sure he understood to some degree, but it was something she must do soon — sit him down and talk to him about herself, about the divorce, about her life now. Later, when there's more time. Carol smiled wryly, knowing full well that she was making excuses to delay the moment.

David stopped to talk to the officer stationed at the entrance desk, and Carol realized with a warm shock that David was proud of her, that he wanted the woman to know that he was her son.

She showed him around, trying to see the desks and offices with his eyes. The place was utilitarian, too crowded with furniture and files and personal things. She noticed that the floor was worn, that the cleaners hadn't wiped down a door where someone had left a smear of what looked like Vegemite.

Carol said, "And this is my office."

The man leaning over her desk straightened quickly.

"Rafe," said Carol, hiding her surprise. "I'd like you to meet my son, David."

Janach seemed unruffled. His sharp face split by a grin, he shook David's hand and asked him how old he was and where he went to school. Carol thought that her son did an admirable job of hiding his boredom at these standard adult questions.

Turning to Carol, Janach said, "I was just dropping off my preliminary report. There's nothing new, I'm afraid. We didn't find anything that would fit the description of the murder weapon. I'd say a crowbar of some sort was used to break open the filing cabinets and could have been used to kill Halstead, but whoever it was took it with him." His smile was subtly patronizing. "Or *her*, if I'm to be politically correct."

When she ignored his remark, Janach went on, "The jerry can's clean. You can buy one in any hardware store, so I'd say there's no point in even trying to trace it. Nothing in the fingerprints of any interest. The usual unidentified partials, but that's standard, as you know. And analysis supports Hanover's findings that gasoline was the accelerant. I'm guessing from the pattern of the fire that the body was drenched, then the remainder of the gas sloshed around the lab and the adjacent office. Then he — or she — stood in the doorway, tossed a match, and got out of there fast."

David, Carol noticed, was listening with attention. When the American paused, David said, "Do you see a lot of dead bodies?"

"A lot," Janach agreed.

"What's the worst one you ever saw?"

"I could show you some photos —"

"No you couldn't," said Carol.

"Aw, Mum!"

After Janach had gone, Carol checked her desk. His report was there on top of the papers. There was no way to tell if he taken the opportunity to look at anything else. She looked through the drawers, but everything seemed to be in order.

"Have you got a new gun? Can I see it?" David asked.

"You can see it, but not touch it."

"Way cool," said David. "Have you killed anyone?"

This was a question she had no intention of answering. "Time for pizza," she announced.

Ursula Vail, graying hair pulled back in a pony-tail, was dressed in what seemed identical black pants and top to those she had worn on Thursday. She met Carol in the rose garden that filled the spacious front yard of the redbrick house. She wore dark glasses with mirror lenses, but Carol suspected that she would still avoid looking directly at anyone.

"How clever of you, Inspector," Ursula piped in her high voice, "to make sure we could be alone. If Bill were here, he'd insist on staying while we talked. You know how men are. They do like to think they're in control."

She gestured toward the garden with one thin hand. "What do you think of my roses?

The bushes were carefully tended, their branches heavy with blooms. They had been planted in a pattern according to color, and each row was a deeper shade. The bushes in the front were white, behind them cream, and so on until the ones near the house were so dark red they almost looked black.

"They're beautiful," said Carol.

Ursula surveyed the roses with a satisfied air. "Not at their best now, but good enough. The secret's in the winter pruning, you know. Have to be ruthless. It's no good if you pussyfoot around."

She led the way around the side of the house, saying over her shoulder, "Thought we'd sit on the patio."

The gardens at the back were also spectacular. Privacy was assured by a border of bushes and small trees, below which tree ferns sheltered. Looking at the massed flowers that crowded the center of the area, many of which she didn't recognize, Carol said, "This is lovely. Do you do all your own gardening?"

"Indeed. My son Tim used to help me, but now that he's overseas, I've coerced Bill into doing any heavy lifting. Everything else is my work." Her upper lip lifted to show a flash of small teeth as she snickered, "Poor dear. I'm afraid I can't let Bill loose near plants, as he doesn't know a weed from a bromeliad."

Directed toward a white metal table and chairs shaded by a large green garden umbrella, Carol reflected that Ursula Vail's fragile build was deceiving. The upkeep of gardens like these would be physically demanding.

"A drink, Inspector? It's fruit juice, of course. I don't imagine you'd consume alcohol while on duty."

"Thank you." Carol waited until Usula had poured them each a glass of reddish liquid, then said, "You mentioned on Thursday that you might be able to help the investigation, and I wonder if you might be able to clear something up."

"If it's about Bill's work, you'll have to ask him."

"Dr. Halstead had an appointment book that he kept himself." Carol waited, but Ursula simply sat very still, watching her.

"There was an entry," Carol went on, "that I thought might refer to you."

"I didn't see him last Wednesday."

"I didn't mention the day."

Ursula picked up her glass, then put it down again. "It wasn't me."

Carol inclined her head in acknowledgment of the denial. She said, "Would you describe what you did on Wednesday."

"Did? Am I a suspect?" Her voice rose on the last syllable to show her indignation.

Carol took out a notebook and pen. "Please."

"Oh, very well," she said with an angry twist to her mouth. "I drove Bill to work — I often do — around eight, and then I came back here and pottered around the garden for the rest of the day. Bill said he'd catch the bus home, so I didn't have to pick him up. I popped out to get something for dinner sometime around five, I think, then came home and spent the rest of the evening here."

"What time did you get back from the shops?"

With an impatient sigh, Ursula said, "I've told you before. About six."

"And your husband?"

"About seven-thirty. Maybe eight."

Carol consulted her notebook. "You did say seven-thirty previously."

"What does it matter!"

"And you maintain you didn't have an appointment with Dr. Halstead that day."

"Inspector, I've no idea why you're harping on

this." Ursula's pale face had flushed a little. "I had no appointment with Brin Halstead."

Carol gave her an apologetic smile. "We have to check these things."

Ursula visibly relaxed. "Of course."

It was interesting, Carol thought, that Ursula Vail didn't ask when the appointment was supposed to be, or why Carol had thought the entry referred to her.

"Now," said Carol conversationally, "I recall you mentioned on Thursday that your husband would be too loyal to reveal everything about Dr. Halstead's activities."

"Bill hasn't been treated justly." The whine in Ursula's voice became more pronounced. "Brin Halstead was always adept at taking all the glory while others did the real work. Now, I'll grant you Brin could charm prospective patients, but he left Bill to come up with wonderful genetic breakthroughs while he took the lion's share of the money and most of the credit. I doubt if there's a patient at the clinic who knows how much is owed to my husband."

Carol said, "Dr. Vail did mention to us that he believed Halstead was in some financial difficulty."

Bitterness crimped her mouth. "He was bleeding the clinic dry! After all that Bill had put into it — to have to watch and see what was happening was almost too much."

Reflecting that Ursula Vail was providing an excellent motive for murder, Carol said, "Your husband and Halstead had a partnership agreement, I presume."

"Oh, yes! With Brin as the controlling partner, of course."

"And in the event of a partner's death . . . ?"

"Do you think Brin would be fair? There should have been a provision in his will that the controlling interest go to Bill, but no! His wife gets it — everything Brin had. The patents, everything! She's unbalanced, you know, so the clinic can go to hell for all she cares."

The note of complaint in her high voice grated so much that Carol wanted to leap to her feet and shake the woman. She took a sip of her drink instead — it had a strange, acid taste — then said, "You mention patents...?"

This was obviously a highly-charged subject for Ursula Vail. Her voice trembled as she said, "The injustice makes me physically ill. Bill developed most of the processes, but Brin sneaked behind his back and applied for patents." She shook her head violently. "I can't talk about it."

After a moment to let Ursula regain her composure, Carol said, "I get the impression, with the client list it has, that the clinic should have been profitable."

"Yes, Inspector, it certainly should have been!" This new outrage seemed to swell Ursula Vail's slight body. "I myself approached Brin and tried to talk some sense into him, but he wouldn't listen. I don't know where the money went, but I suspect Brin had been living beyond his means for quite some time. Of course, Leta spends money like it's going out of fashion."

"Could Halstead's problems be linked to blackmail?" asked Carol delicately.

Ursula sniffed. "I suppose you mean that item on the news this morning about IVF problems. It's rubbish. Not true. There's nothing in that story to hurt the clinic."

"But Dr. Halstead could have substituted his own sperm, had he wanted to? And none of his clients would be the wiser?"

Ursula clicked her tongue irritably. "That's obvious, but I can't imagine Brin being so stupid."

"In summary," said Carol, "would I be correct in saying there was considerable tension between your husband and Brin Halstead?"

Ursula obviously saw this as a loaded question. She hesitated, then said, "Not exactly." She took a long swallow from her glass, then refilled it from the jug. "I won't pretend there weren't some issues, as there are in any business partnership, but on a personal level there was no real animosity. For example, Brin put in a good word for our son, Tim, when he wanted to study medicine overseas. Made sure he got into the best medical school."

"Is he your only child?"

"Yes." She rubbed her forehead, hard, and a red mark appeared on her pale skin. "We had a daughter, Melanie, but she died when she was only five. Drowned in a swimming pool." She glanced briefly toward the garden. "I had it filled in."

"I'm so sorry." Carol said the words automatically, fascinated by the expression of glittering rage that had appeared on Ursula Vail's thin face.

"Sorry? Not as sorry as we are. If we'd known the advances that were going to be made, we could have done something. Bill blames himself, I know, but I said to him, no one can predict what will happen in fifteen years. No one."

She snatched up her glass, took a mouthful, then slapped it down so hard that juice slopped over onto the white metal of the table.

"There have been startling medical advances ..." said Carol, fishing.

"Advances beyond our wildest dreams. If it had only happened later, we would have done what the Alarics have. They'll have their son again, but Melanie is gone forever."

Carol said, "I've been told that Faye Pickerson is carrying the Alarics' child." She saw herself reflected in the mirrored glasses as Ursula turned her head.

"Faye Pickerson," said Ursula, "is carrying Conrad Alaric. Surely you've realized. When Leta killed her brother, before they turned off the life support, Iniga and Perry had Brin take cells and freeze them. It's Conrad, or, if you prefer, his clone, that the surrogate has in her belly."

CHAPTER ELEVEN

Bourke called when she was getting into her car. When she told him what Ursula Vail had said, he snorted his disbelief. "A clone of a dead son? I don't believe it."

"From what Leta Halstead said in my office, neither does she, but if the Alarics just *think* it's true, it seems to remove a motive for either of them to kill their son-in-law."

"While you were having these amazing revelations from Ursula Vail," said Bourke, plainly irritated, "*I* was wasting my time with her husband. He had an insurance assessor there, and I was supposed to traipse around with them, no doubt to add a touch of authenticity to the outrageous claims of damage Vail's making."

"What sort of claims?"

"For one thing, he says that almost all of the samples in the liquid oxygen container have been contaminated. There was much argument between him and the insurance guy as to what dollar value could be placed on such things as human tissue."

"Odd," said Carol. "Tom Lorant told me he didn't think anything had been tampered with. Perhaps we'd better ask him a few more questions on the topic."

"I did get one bit of information," said Bourke. "Apparently one of the clinic's clients is talking legal action. The insurance guy was quite excited about it — seems it's the talk of his office."

"You got a name?"

"James Neale. He's a junior partner in a large law firm. Even more interesting, his address just happens to be the same as Tom Lorant's."

"Give me twenty minutes and I'll meet you there."

Lorant's street was on a steep hill, his nondescript little two-story terrace seeming to lean against its neighbors for strength. Bourke was waiting for her, leaning against his car.

"You look pleased with yourself," she said.

"Just as I got here, someone was pulling away from this spot in front of Lorant's place. Don't think she saw me, but I had a good look at her. It was Elaine Kaynes, and you know, she was driving a white car."

A stranger to Carol opened the door when Bourke

rang the bell. He was stocky, with solid shoulders and a thick chest. He wore ancient shorts and a striped shirt so laundered that the colors were barely discernible. He had straight sandy hair and heavy pale growth on his arms and legs.

"Yes?"

Bourke gave their names. "We were hoping to see Thomas Lorant."

The man jutted his prominent jaw. "Can you prove you're who you say you are?"

He studied the identification for each with unhurried attention. "Right, so you're the cops. Why should I let you through the front door? Have you got a warrant?"

"Oh, for God's sake, James!" called a voice from within the house. "Let them in!"

James stood back, his mouth tight. "You heard him."

Thomas Lorant, also barefoot and in shorts, was lounging on a settee upholstered in gold and white. The same colors were repeated in the room, which had a fragile air about it, as though the furniture might break under the weight of the owners' sturdy physicality.

James sat down beside Lorant and stared at Carol and Bourke. He didn't offer them a seat.

"This is stupid," said Tom Lorant, heaving himself up. "Come to the back, where we can be comfortable."

As they were seated at the broad kitchen table, Carol glanced around the room. Clean lines and primary colors — blue and yellow — made the kitchen cheerfully bright. There was no clutter. Even the hanging plants seemed disciplined.

Unasked, James provided mugs of coffee. Then he settled down beside Lorant and fixed them with a blank stare. He had small deep blue eyes under sandy eyebrows.

"Meet James Neale," said Lorant.

"What do you want?" said James.

Bourke took out his notebook. "A few questions."

"I suppose you think I should have told you I was gay," said Lorant to Carol, "but it's none of your damn business." His voice was soft, but the resentment showed.

"Everything's our damn business when there's a murder," said Carol, her tone pleasant.

Under his mustache Lorant's teeth showed in a grudging smile. "The secular equivalent of a confessional, eh? Tell all and your soul will be clean."

"Sergeant Bourke's just come from the clinic," said Carol. "It appears Dr. Vail has decided that a fair proportion of the material kept in liquid nitrogen has been tampered with. At least, that's what he's telling the insurance assessor."

Lorant didn't seem surprised. "Yeah, he would. He's getting rid of evidence, Inspector. He hasn't got the guts that Brin had, isn't willing to go to the edge of research and beyond. I'd say that Vail's terrified there'll be a medical audit, that he'll get it in the neck. And that stuff on the news this morning about IVF irregularities will have really stirred him up."

"With Dr. Halstead dead, I presume the clinic itself will be the target of any lawsuits."

"There won't be much joy there," said Lorant. "I'm sure you know the financial situation, Inspector. Bill Vail will throw up his hands and say that, being the junior partner, he knew nothing about anything irregular, and then he'll let the company go to the wall, wait a while, and start up again." He grunted. "I'll give him this, he's a damned good genetic technician."

"Do you know anything about taking patents out on any of the genetic procedures?"

Lorant raised a shoulder. "That's the business side of things. Nothing to do with me. Bill Vail might know."

"He's a prick," said James, "him and his bloody wife."

"Now that the shit is really starting to hit the fan," said Lorant, "it's really an advantage to Vail that he can blame Halstead for everything that's wrong at the clinic."

Wryly amused at this blatant attempt to suggest Vail might be a murderer, Carol said, "You're saying Dr. Vail killed Brin Halstead?"

"I'm just saying it's convenient, Inspector. That's all."

Carol made eye contact with Bourke, who said to James, "Tell us about Cindy Farr."

James glanced at Lorant, then back at Carol and Bourke. "She's a surrogate for us. It's a business arrangement. That's all there is to it."

"Which one of you is the father?"

Again the look. James said to Bourke, "I am. What of it?"

"And is Cindy Farr the mother?"

"What possible interest can this be to you?" asked Lorant, moving impatiently in his chair. "Look, I'm sick of this whole conversation. Let's get this straight, and you can get out of here. The egg came from an anonymous donor at the clinic. She was given fertility drugs, which encourage ovulation, and she was kind enough to donate eggs that she didn't use. I don't know who she is, and I couldn't find out if I tried. The embryo was implanted in Cindy Farr. She's being paid, and paid well, for the pregnancy."

While Bourke asked more questions about the procedure and the Halstead Clinic's system of protecting the names of donors, Carol studied the two across the table. It was normal to see people nervous or confused when questioned by the police, even when they had nothing to hide. These two men were hostile, she understood that, but there was something else beneath the surface.

When Bourke paused, Carol said, "We were told that you weren't happy with the surrogate process."

"We weren't happy with the cost," said James Neale. "We paid through the nose. Otherwise, everything's okay."

"You didn't consider cloning?"

"No." Lorant was decisive. "Works well with sheep and mice, but not humans."

Carol raised her eyebrows. "We've been told that Brin Halstead was actively selling the procedure to the gay community, and that there are at least two cloned fetuses in existence."

Lorant shrugged. "That was Brin's con job," said Lorant. "We're years away from successful human cloning."

Bourke asked James Neale, "Why are you suing the Halstead Clinic?"

"None of your business," he glowered. "It'll be settled out of court. You don't need to know anything about it."

"We need to know," said Carol.

She waited patiently. At last James said, "It was breach of contract. That's all I'm saying."

Bourke said, "The guy from the insurance company said considerably more. As I recall, he said it was a ground-breaking case and his company wasn't a bit happy about it."

"Tell them," said Tom Lorant, his voice weary. "They'll find out anyway."

James swore under his breath, then said, "The last time Cindy Farr went to our obstetrician, we got her to agree for a sample to be taken for DNA typing. Tom was starting to worry that Halstead had lied to us, and this was the only way to find out for sure."

"And the baby isn't yours?" said Bourke.

"Oh, the baby's *mine*." A muscle jumped in James Neale's jaw. "The trouble is — it's someone else's too."

Carol sat back in her chair. "So you did believe at first that your clone had been implanted?"

Lorant spread his hands. "James has a far better genetic profile than I have, so we decided to use his sperm. You can ignore what I said before. Cloning of mammals isn't far off in the future — it's happening now, even without the proper scientific protocols of testing on primates first. I believed Brin Halstead when he showed me how he'd succeeded with human cells. He offered the procedure to us, and we took it."

"Mortgaged the bloody house to do it," said James.

Carol took a sip of her coffee and found it half cold. "A few minutes ago, you said you would never consider cloning."

Lorant gave her a sour smile. "Inspector, as of this moment it's against the law. I don't want to be an example of a little guy fighting the system. I don't want us on the cover of every bloody magazine. I just want to be happy. To have a family with James and our son."

"Suing the clinic doesn't seem to be a way to avoid publicity," observed Bourke.

"Halstead would have settled," James ground out. "The bastard didn't want something like this to get out, or all the others he's sold on cloning might start to ask uncomfortable questions."

Carol said, "There was another case settled out of court."

"Yeah, Daris and his wife got a hell of a lot of money, but that wasn't cloning, it was a normal IVF —" Lorant grinned "— except that the kid wasn't related to either of them. Word is, the father was Halstead, and the mother an anonymous donor."

"Who tipped Daris off? There didn't seem to be any reason for him to have a DNA test done on the baby."

Lorant paused, then said, "It was Elaine. And she got paid for it, under the table."

There was a moment's silence. Carol heard the motor of the refrigerator cut in. Somewhere in a neighboring house a baby cried.

"Speaking of Elaine Kaynes, why was she here this afternoon?"

Lorant answered a little too quickly. "She wasn't."

"I saw her," said Bourke.

"Jesus!" James slammed his chair back and got to his feet. Ramming his fists into the pockets of his shorts, he began to move aimlessly about the kitchen.

Lorant watched him for a few moments, then said to Carol, "Elaine came here to tell us that she'd talked to *The Shipley Report* people about us. We'll be mentioned in the program coming up, not by name, but anyone who knows us can put two and two together. She even tried to persuade us to go on the show." He snorted. "Generous expenses, she said."

"And what did you say to this?"

James gave a bark of laughter. "I said we'd sue."

CHAPTER TWELVE

The surf was low, slapping halfheartedly onto the beige sand. The breeze from the sea had a welcome briskness after the heat of the day. Carol and Sybil walked side by side along the edge of the water where the surface was firm under their bare feet. Seagulls, arrogant and pushy, congregated in small, quarrelsome groups near the boundary of the foam, or glided, shrieking, overhead. The beach curved in a huge pale crescent, bracketed at each end with tumbled sandstone rocks, above which reared weathered cliffs in whose profiles Carol fancied she could trace frowning, ancient faces.

"This is heaven," said Carol, taking in a deep breath of salty air. She looked across at Sybil, who caught her glance and smiled.

The cloak of contentment that Carol felt settle around her was ephemeral but comforting. Sybil, her red hair flaming in the setting sun, was at once familiar and provokingly strange. Looking beside her at the woman with white jeans rolled up to her knees and loose-limbed stride, Carol felt suddenly that they had never really known each other. That there were delightful surprises, paradoxes, mysteries, yet to be explored.

Impulsively, Carol said, "Have you ever wanted children?"

"You're getting hung up on this Halstead case, Carol."

Reaching over to brush her fingers, Carol said, "Have you?"

"I've thought about it lots of times, but no, I don't think so."

"Not with Tony?"

Sybil gave her a look she couldn't decipher. They had rarely talked of Sybil's husband, and Carol knew it was in a way bizarre to do so now, since he had been flung to his death from a cliff only a kilometer along the coast from where they were walking.

"Especially not with Tony." Sybil's voice held a warning note.

They went along a few more paces. Carol paused to pick up a starfish and throw it back into the sea. "I suppose it's this whole fertility clinic thing," she said. She wanted to tell Sybil about Pat and Mark Bourke, but that would be a betrayal of a confidence. "You can have your eggs frozen and use them years later," Carol said.

"You're worrying about my biological clock? It's ticking faster, I admit, but it's my prerogative to be concerned about it, isn't it?"

Carol abruptly felt distanced from her, as though a shadow had fallen between them. "Darling, I didn't mean . . ."

"What's the matter, Carol? Is it something to do with David?"

"It's nothing to do with David." She wondered if that were true. The Halstead case had driven home to her the lengths to which so many people would go to have children to raise. She felt that at some level her son must believe that she was an unnatural mother, that she had almost casually abandoned him.

Even in the abstract, a mother walking away from her child was shocking to Carol. And she had done it. She could never explain to David the acid pain, the gulf of emptiness, the texture of despair that had gone with that bitterly regretted decision.

"Mark and I interviewed a surrogate mother today."

"Where are you going with this, Carol?"

Carol stopped and faced her, arms wide. "I don't know."

Sybil smiled. "That's a first!"

You pierced my heart with that smile, thought Carol. She wanted to mock herself for being mushy, but couldn't.

They didn't speak again until they had reached

the rocks at the end of the beach and turned back. "I'd like to see David sometime over Christmas," said Carol.

Sybil shoved her hands into the back pockets of her jeans. "He's very welcome here. We could have a barbecue. Do you think he'd like to ask some of his friends?"

"We could have a barbecue at my house."

Carol's statement fell to the sand and kept on sinking. She counted the steps — five, six, seven — before Sybil answered.

"I can't go back there."

"Never?"

"I don't think so."

Drop it, Carol thought, but she heard herself pleading, "When enough time has passed . . ."

"There'll never be enough time." Sybil's voice was quiet, reasonable. "I know you love that house, and you can cope with what happened there, but I can't."

"But I told you, I'll change everything. Not just the furniture, I'll have it rebuilt."

"It would still be the same place. I believed I was going to die, and when he made me swallow that stuff, when he held my nose until I opened my mouth . . ."

Carol couldn't bear to hear it. The images of what she had seen when she had walked into her house that day were still corrosively vivid. "Sybil, I understand, really I do."

Carol heard her sigh. Sybil said, "Intellectually, I can process it. I'm aware that what happened was because of coincidence and plain bad luck and that it's over. I know the standard formula, that one accepts it and forgets it. But I can't tell my body to behave in this sensible, businesslike way. I just cannot go back there."

There was a taut silence between them until they reached the point where they turned to cross the width of the dry sand and head for Sybil's home.

Sybil said, "You could move here, to the beach."

"I could."

"Would you sell the Seaforth house?"

A protest rose in her throat. "I grew up there," Carol said. "I've added to it, changed it. And the outlook is so beautiful . . ."

"You sound like a real estate agent."

"I don't think I can sell it."

"And living here?"

Carol raised her shoulders. "I don't know."

"Okay, Carol."

"Don't say okay like that! You make me feel that I have to choose."

Anger flared in Sybil's face. "Is it so hard? Your house or me?"

"Don't be ridiculous."

"Let's drop it, shall we? Talk about it some other time."

Carol had the feeling that everything was dribbling away, like sand through her fingers. "You know I love you," she said.

"That isn't the issue."

"A *balmy* night," said Sybil. "It looks such a stupid word when it's written down, but it sounds like it is."

The evening air was sweet and soft. Carol pushed her empty plate away and stretched. The smell of hot barbecue and the perfume of climbing honeysuckle blended into a delicious scent. "I cannot eat another bite," she said.

Sybil's backyard was private, screened by native bushes and high fences overgrown with a choko vine so luxuriant that it threatened to bring down the structure. The flickering torches were supposed to discourage mosquitoes, but Carol had already felt several infuriating pricks on her bare skin.

Jeffrey sat on the flagstone near them, washing with care his ginger face. That done, he put one back leg in the air in a position only a cat could make graceful and began to groom his nether regions.

He looked up suddenly, and, following his intent gaze, Carol saw a blurred feathery movement as something swooped soundlessly across the yard. "An owl," she said, pleased, but with an odd flutter of alarm.

What was the old superstition? *I heard the owl call my name.* If you heard that, you were fated to die.

Carol looked across at Sybil's shadowed face and raised her wineglass in a toast. "To us?"

"Don't make it a question," said Sybil, smiling. "Unless you have some doubts."

"No doubts." Carol knew she had spoken too quickly, too emphatically.

But it's true, she thought. Just at this moment, when we aren't worrying about the future or the past. She slapped at another mosquito. "We'll have to go inside — the mozzies are feasting on me."

In the kitchen, plates and barbecue implements piled high in her hands, Carol said, "Darling, let's go to bed. Now, this minute."

"We have to at least clean our teeth," said Sybil, laughing. "I'm a woman with standards, however swept away by lust."

Toothbrush in hand, Carol stared at her own reflection in the mirror of the guest bathroom. *I'll show you how much I love you,* she thought, knowing all the time that it was a futile task.

That Carol loved Sybil and delighted in her body was not, as Sybil had said, the issue. Nor that Carol embraced with elation Sybil's mind, her laughter, her own unassailable, distinct self. That wasn't a question.

Carol's face looked back at her, contained, cool. She knew the answer but didn't want to consider it. She tried the word: *commitment.* Commitment full and absolute.

"Psychobabble," she said to her reflection.

It was comforting to dismiss it with a derisive label, and a greater comfort too, when a few moments later all thought was submerged in the touch of Sybil's skin, the heat of her willing mouth.

The intensity of their lovemaking always surprised Carol. They had kissed a thousand times before, but each time, it seemed, she found it sweeter, deeper. Pleasure, joy, leaped in her, crowding out the doubts, the images that had the power to hurt, the fear that, after all, they would not stay together.

They knew how to play each other's body, knew how to prolong the inexorable tension until it became an agony, an ecstasy shrieking to be released. Tonight she would take Sybil, would take herself, to somewhere they had never been.

"Carol," said Sybil, arching beneath her.

Carol laughed with joy. "Ah, darling," she said. "Anything you want, I'll do anything for you."

CHAPTER THIRTEEN

Sunday morning was delightfully decadent. Sybil threw on some clothes and drove to the local bakery for hot, buttery croissants while Carol padded naked around the kitchen making coffee and assuaging Jeffrey's cries for attention.

When Sybil returned, they went back to bed with the Sunday paper, croissants, and coffee. Then they made laughing love among the crumbs and crumpled pages.

Later, driving to the appointment with Faye Pickerson, Carol found herself frowning. The evening, the morning, had been wonderful, carefree, like a holiday. Tonight Carol would go back to her own house, and find Sinker, although well provided for by the next-door neighbor, ostentatiously sulking, and she would spend time soothing his hurt feelings. If only Sybil and Jeffrey could come home...

That was it. Home. The Seaforth house was that, and more, to Carol, no matter what had happened there. But for Sybil, it could never be a comforting home again.

There were quiet, pleasant streets off the main arteries of West Ryde. Carol checked her street directory and turned off to find a suburban Eden. A typical Sunday afternoon. People were washing cars in driveways, and kids rode bicycles along the footpaths. Carol could imagine neighbors chatting across the back fences, pulling together when someone in a family was ill, and sending postcards to everyone on the block when on holiday. Of course, she thought sardonically, this was just her fantasy. In reality, she supposed, the same problems that beset people everywhere were here behind the neat fences and well-kept front gardens.

Faye Pickerson's house was just as anonymously agreeable as all the rest. There was nothing arresting about the building or the prosaic front garden. A light blue sedan, obviously new, sat in the driveway. For once she had beaten Bourke, so Carol parked and waited, listening to the neighborhood sounds: the racket of a lawnmower, the sharp bark of a dog; the shouts of kids in a backyard pool.

"Sorry I'm late." Bourke was at her window, his face creased with concern. "The traffic was worse than I thought."

Carol had never understood his pathological worry about punctuality, and how being just a little late for something could disturb him so much.

"Hey, it's Sunday," she said. "Relax."

Sunday or not, Faye Pickerson wasn't relaxed. She had a pale, freckled face and a V of lines between her eyes. Carol knew she was twenty-eight, but she looked much younger. She wore a brown maternity smock and a short black skirt that showed her spindly legs. "I haven't done anything wrong," she said in a reedy voice as soon as she opened the door. "My mum can tell you that."

This was not strictly true. Alerted by Cindy Farr's comment, Bourke had run a check on Faye Pickerson. She had two convictions for shoplifting and had served time for one scheme, also involving her mother, where elderly pensioners were defrauded. Both of them had been clean for several years — or, Carol thought, perhaps it was that they hadn't been caught.

Faye's mother, also pale and freckled but considerably larger in every way, loomed over her daughter's shoulder. "Picking on people, that's what you cops do," she said loudly. "You should be ashamed of yourselves."

Faye seemed content to let her mother do the talking. "Thelma Pickerson's the name," the woman said, impatiently gesturing for Carol and Bourke to enter. She wore a voluminous off-white house dress.

"And don't hang about out there. Don't want the neighbors talking."

Carol gazed around yet another sitting room. Her life, she thought whimsically, was measured out in other people's houses, sitting on other people's furniture.

This particular room was as pedestrian as the outside of the house. Every item seemed to be chosen for its commonplace dullness. There were no bright colors — everything was in neutral shades, including the clothing of the two women. Their expressions showed that they regarded Carol and Bourke as intruders. Thelma's attitude was militant; Faye's, anxious.

Carol said, "We're so sorry to disturb you on a Sunday."

"Sorry, are you?" asked Thelma. "Then why are you here?"

"When did you last see Dr. Halstead?" said Bourke to Faye. His tone was unexpectedly gentle.

"Why, Tuesday," she said, unguarded. "Yes, Tuesday it was. On the phone. He was just checking to see if I was okay."

Her mother cast her daughter a whiplash look. "We've got nothing to say," she said to Carol. "We know our rights."

"We're investigating a murder," said Carol.

Faye put her hand to her mouth. Carol noticed the fingernails were bitten to the quick. Faye murmured, "I can't believe it. Dr. Halstead was so nice."

Carol had often wondered why people said that, as

141

though niceness was some protection against murderous anger or greed.

Bourke leaned forward, speaking to Faye. "We know it's upsetting, but it could help our inquiries if you'd answer just a few questions."

"Faye doesn't know anything."

Carol smiled at the mother. "You've met Dr. Halstead?"

Thelma drew back, suspicious. "Of course! Do you think I'd let Faye get involved with something if I didn't know every last thing about it?"

"And you were quite happy for your daughter to be a surrogate?" Bourke asked.

Thelma examined this question of Bourke's for hidden criticism, and, apparently finding none, said, "Why shouldn't Faye help someone who can't have a baby? She's a healthy girl, and she's lucky that she feels terrific when she's pregnant." She looked to her daughter for confirmation. "Don't you?"

Faye nodded. "Well, it's not much to do, really. Just a bit uncomfortable near the end. I don't have trouble delivering." She glanced around the room. "And we've got this nice house and everything, haven't we, Mum?"

Bourke said, with a look of genuine inquiry, "I've wondered how you get into this line of work."

"It's quite aboveboard," said Thelma with a bellicose glare. "Just what are you suggesting?"

"I'd really like to know."

Carol was interested to see how Bourke's plain statement convinced her. "All right then," she said. She nodded to her daughter. "You tell him."

"Well, I had a baby when I was fifteen. I know

it's the fashion to keep them now, but I was just too young, so I put her up for adoption. That's how I knew I wouldn't have any trouble with a pregnancy. And then I saw this ad a few years ago — or rather, my aunt saw it — and I went in, and it looked like a good job, so I took it."

"My sister's a nurse," said Thelma. "The ad was in one of the medical magazines she gets."

"The baby you're carrying now," Carol said to Faye, "it's for the Alarics, isn't it?"

Thelma bristled. "What's it to you?"

"Just background information," said Carol smoothly.

"It's a boy," said Faye. "That's all I know. I'm not interested, really. I mean, I'll never have anything to do with the baby once it's born. It's someone else's, not mine."

Carol could see from Bourke's expression that he was having trouble accepting this philosophy. Before he could make a comment, Carol said, "What do you know about cloning?"

Her question drew two uncomprehending stares. "Cloning?" said Thelma. "Isn't that something to do with that sheep?"

"Yes, it is," said Carol, dismissing the subject. "The Alarics have been very good to you, haven't they?"

"They want the best for the child," said Thelma, narrowing her eyes as if Carol were implying something underhanded. "She couldn't do it herself, you know — get pregnant and carry a baby. She's much too old."

"Iniga Alaric, you mean?"

Thelma nodded. "Stuck up," she said. "Thinks she doesn't show it, but I can see she believes she's better than us."

"Mrs. Alaric is ever so nice," said Faye. "She rented this house for us, and we got new furniture. And she bought me a car and everything."

Carol asked, "Do you see Mr. Alaric?"

Faye's mother gave a sharp laugh. "He's the one that pays all the bills, so he wants to see where his money's going. I reckon he's over here more often than she is."

"And Leta," said Faye. "She's *really* nice."

"You mean Dr. Halstead's wife?"

"What is it with you cops?" said Thelma. "Don't you ever listen?"

Carol looked at her with polite inquiry. "Did Dr. Halstead ever accompany his wife on her visits?"

"No, never," said Faye. "But Mr. and Mrs. Alaric came with her most times."

"So Leta Halstead and her parents came here together?"

"There you go again," said Thelma. "She just said that, didn't she?"

On a sudden hunch, Carol asked Faye, "And who else from the Halstead Clinic has visited?"

"She's not really from the clinic, but Cindy's been here a couple of times."

"Troublemaker, that Farr girl. Always has been," announced Thelma Pickerson.

Faye went on, "And there's that lady from the clinic —"

She broke off when her mother made a warning noise.

"What lady?" asked Bourke, smiling persuasively. When Faye hesitated, he added, "This *is* an official investigation."

"Leave her alone," commanded her mother. "I'll tell you. It was Dr. Halstead's assistant, Gilda. Gilda Milton. He used to send her to check that everything was okay."

"And there was that reporter . . ."

Thoroughly disgusted, Thelma snapped, "For heaven's sake, Faye! Keep your mouth shut."

"Someone from *The Shipley Report*?"

Thelma dismissed Bourke's question with an irritated grunt. "Not TV. I suppose I might as well tell you, since you'll badger me until I do." She heaved herself up and went over to a small cabinet. "She left a business card. It's here, somewhere . . ." She rummaged through a drawer. "Here." She handed it to Carol.

The card was embossed with a name, *Noelle Winthall*, business and private telephone numbers, a mobile phone, and an e-mail address.

Carol said, "Ms. Winthall was working with Dr. Halstead on a book, I believe."

"Really?" said Thelma. "Then it's a bit odd, isn't it, that she asked us not to mention to anyone, particularly Dr. Halstead, that she'd been to see us?"

"Yeah," said Faye with a sly smile, "and she made it worth our while to keep quiet, didn't she, Mum?"

Her mother glared. "You'll talk your way into an early grave, my girl," she said.

* * * * *

When the front door slammed behind them, Bourke said, "Popular place. Must be the hospitable atmosphere."

"Must be," agreed Carol. "Certainly a lot of people have been very interested to see this particular surrogate mother."

"Do *you* think she's carrying the clone of Conrad Alaric?" It was clear that Bourke didn't subscribe to this view.

Carol shook her head. "I've no idea, but a DNA test would settle the matter one way or the other, so we need to know if one's been done. A cell sample can be taken during a standard medical examination, so Faye wouldn't necessarily know anything about it. You could try contacting her obstetrician, though patient-doctor confidentiality will be an issue."

She turned Noelle Winthall's card over in her fingers. Reluctantly, Thelma Pickerson had relinquished it, after making a show of copying down the numbers, saying, "In case we might need them."

"I'd say Ma Pickerson will be on the phone to her as soon as she thinks things through," said Bourke. "Could be a good idea to see Noelle Winthall this afternoon, if she's home."

He came back from his car phone triumphant. "Got her on her car phone on their way back from the beach. They'll meet us in half an hour."

Noelle Winthall and Beth Chu lived in an apartment in a luxurious building on the northern shore of the harbor at Wollstonecraft. "Cost a bit," said

Bourke as they stood at the security gate. "Journalism must pay better than I thought."

The view from the apartment was one that was new to Carol. She had never seen Sydney Harbour from this particular aspect. She leaned across the railing of the tiled deck that overlooked Balls Head Bay and picked out familiar landmarks from an unfamiliar angle.

"This is beautiful," she said.

"Have you been here long?" asked Bourke.

"I married a rich woman," said Noelle, apparently feeling the need to explain.

Beth Chu smiled. "Not so rich," she said. She was in contrast to the tall, athletic Noelle, being slight and soft, with a gentle, sweet voice. Her hair was straight and very black, and her dark eyes were alert, as though she wanted to make sure she missed nothing. She was obviously pregnant, and Carol remembered that Noelle had said the twins were due in March.

"Come back to the sitting room," said Noelle, "and have a beer." She put up a hand. "Don't tell me you won't drink on duty — it's just a beer."

"Okay," said Carol. She rarely drank beer, but she was thirsty, and the thought of the cool amber liquid was enticing. She was amused to see Bourke's grateful glance.

"I'd kill for a cold one," he said.

The little sitting room had sliding doors that opened into a tiny courtyard. "Our backyard," said Noelle with a flourish.

The beer was delicious. Carol took a long swallow

and put down the can. "This could be seen as bribing a police officer," she said.

Noelle, sitting beside Beth on a steel-framed settee with green-and-cream striped cushions, grinned widely. "Do I need to bribe you?"

"What do you know about Faye Pickerson?" said Bourke.

"She's a surrogate for the Halstead Clinic." Noelle's reply sounded open, frank.

"Have you met her?'

"Why yes. Yes, I have."

Carol smiled at her. "Did Thelma Pickerson call you this afternoon?"

Noelle exchanged a look with Beth, then said, "She got me on the car phone, just after Sergeant Bourke called."

"And what did she say?"

Noelle tilted her head. "Nothing much. She doesn't like the cops, you know. Wanted to warn me that you knew that I'd been there."

Beth said firmly, "Noelle had every right to see them. She was interviewing Thelma and Faye for the book she was writing with Dr. Halstead."

"Yes," said Bourke, "but it was to be written *with* Dr. Halstead, so why pay the Pickersons to keep the fact that you'd been talking to them quiet?"

Noelle sank back. She reached for Beth's hand, and linked their fingers. "We thought something might be wrong. I'd got the feeling that Halstead might have conned me about cloning a cell from a dead person. Faye's pregnancy, if it really is the clone of Conrad Alaric, will make my book a best-seller, worldwide."

Noting that Noelle had entirely appropriated the

book to her name, Carol wondered if there had been a contract between her and Halstead, and, if so, what would happen now that he was dead. "And have you found out?" Carol asked.

Noelle beamed. "It's true. The baby will be a clone of the Alarics' dead son."

Skepticism clear on his face, Bourke said, "How do you know that for sure?"

"I saw a copy of the DNA lab report. I'm a journalist. I've got my sources."

"How long ago was this?"

"Three, four weeks." She broke off to frown at Bourke. "You're not going to let this out, are you? God, there'll be media braying in the streets if you do. I've got an exclusive, and there's no way I'm going to share *this* story!"

"Who requested the DNA test?" said Carol. "The Alarics?"

"Not them — they've always taken everything Brin Halstead told them as gospel. I thought it was odd, really, until I realized she must be worried about inheritance. I mean, her parents have lots of money, but she's going to have to share, isn't she?"

"Leta Halstead?" Carol was more than surprised. "*She* arranged the test?"

"Leta Halstead," said Noelle.

CHAPTER FOURTEEN

When Carol came into the office early on Monday morning, there was an urgent message from Iniga Alaric. She put down her briefcase, checked through her other messages, then called the number given.

Iniga Alaric answered at the second ring. "Inspector Ashton, I must see you as soon as possible."

"Is there some problem?"

"I'll discuss it when we meet. Can you be here at nine?"

After she'd disconnected, Carol sat thinking for a

moment, then found Joan Yaller's card. As she had hoped, the professor was in her university office early. "Good morning, Inspector Ashton, what can I do for you?"

"I gather it's possible to patent genetic procedures."

"Yes, it is. In fact, personally I find recent developments most disturbing in this area. Giant industrial companies, particularly overseas, are pouring millions into genetic research and genetics-based technologies, obviously hoping to get in at the ground floor as far as the coming age of genetic commerce is concerned. They could be mass-producing a range of customized, cloned animals within a few years."

Carol was beginning to see why Ursula Vail was so angry about the patents she claimed Halstead had stolen from her husband. "So if someone patented a new cloning technique it could be worth a fortune?"

"A fortune doesn't even come close to describing it. For example, here in Australia we have a biotech company that has applied for a patent with regard to a new cloning technique it has pioneered. It's likely the patent will not only cover the process itself, but it will also cover any cloned animals resulting from it."

Carol thanked the professor for her time and put down the receiver thoughtfully. Motives for Brin Halstead's murder seemed to proliferate with every passing day, but the eternal themes of anger and greed seemed to underlie them all.

After dealing with a few administrative matters, Carol quickly read through the preliminary financial report on Halstead that Maureen Oatland had left on top of the pile in the in-tray. Then she set off for the rarefied world of Double Bay. It was only a short drive from her office, but a long way in income and social influence.

As she negotiated the traffic, she thought about the coverage of the case in the newspaper she'd read over breakfast. The details of the postmortem had obviously been leaked to the reporter, and the article had contained considerable speculation about the IVF program Halstead had been running, including some well-informed conjectures about cloning.

She'd left a message for Mark Bourke, who was at the clinic checking through files with Gilda Milton to winnow names of other clients who might have reason to be angry with Brin Halstead. After reading the coverage of the Halstead murder this morning, the fact that she found Janach apparently checking out her desk on Saturday now looked a little suspicious. She was reluctant to consider that he might be the source for some of the information turning up in the media, but it was a possibility. It wouldn't hurt to take precautions, and Carol wanted Bourke to be careful with any material he was collecting on the case.

The Alarics' house sheltered behind tall stone walls, its entrance gate a masterpiece of wrought iron, its security system state of the art. Screened, identified, and finally permitted to enter, Carol parked on the gravel drive and went to the massive, studded door.

The woman in black who answered her ring would not have been out of place in an old black-and-white movie. Carol was immediately reminded of Mrs. Danvers in *Rebecca*. The house, too, was rather like a movie set. She glanced up at the curving staircase as they passed it, thinking that it was perfect for a grand entrance. They passed room after room, Carol's footsteps echoing on the stone floor — the woman had shoes that made no noise — until they reached a conservatory filled with orchids of, it seemed, every possible variety. The air was hot and humid, and the pervading smell of damp soil filled the air.

Coming forward to greet her, Iniga Alaric gestured toward the banks of orchids. "You like these?" She was wearing a pale gray silk suit and a heavy strand of creamy pearls. Her honey-blond hair was perfect, her makeup flawless. She appeared ready, even at this early hour, to go out to meet similarly attired society matrons for lunch.

Carol murmured something polite, although she had never warmed to orchids. With their sophisticated petals they had a haughty, patronizing air that was somehow alien.

Iniga turned a full circle, surveying the contents of the conservatory. "My husband's hobby. He spends more time, I fear, with these plants than with me."

Under her light cotton jacket, Carol felt perspiration run down her ribs. "You said it was urgent."

"My dear Inspector, of course. I mustn't waste your valuable time." Iniga led the way to a glass-walled alcove furnished with wooden garden chairs. The cushions were covered with dull green vinyl and looked sticky, as though they, too, were sweating. "It's a little hot so close to the conservatory, but Janet will bring us something cool to drink."

Carol sank into the chair and immediately felt hotter and more uncomfortable. The woman in black appeared with a tray containing a thermal jug, glasses, and a plate of tiny, sugared buns. She set the tray down on a circular table, and waited to be dismissed. This Iniga Alaric did with a casual wave of her hand.

"Do help yourself to iced coffee," said Iniga.

She watched as Carol poured the liquid into a heavy crystal glass. At once, condensation began to bead its sides. "Do you know Dr. Naomi Reed?" she asked, obviously expecting Carol to answer in the affirmative.

"The psychiatrist? Yes, we've met."

"Dear Naomi," said Iniga. "She's such a help in an emergency. There's no good way to say this, but I'm afraid my daughter's had a nervous breakdown. Naomi — she's a close personal friend — admitted Leta to her hospital yesterday afternoon. She must have complete rest — no visitors."

On two occasions Carol had visited patients at Naomi Reed's private hospital. She had a mental picture of the pastel walls, carpeted halls, and huge bowls of fresh flowers at intervals. The extensive gardens could be seen from almost every discreetly barred window, and solicitous white-coated staff spoke in quiet, attentive tones.

"I'm very sorry to hear that."

"Frankly, Inspector, I wasn't surprised, though it was a dreadful blow to Perry. He thought Leta was quite over that. As a child, you know, she was . . . unhappy."

Carol could feel perspiration on her face, though Iniga Alaric looked serenely cool. Opting to be direct,

Carol said, "Are you saying your daughter attempted to harm herself?"

"Sleeping tablets. I'd like to think it was a mistake, that she got confused and took too many, but in the past . . ." Her voice trailed off, her expression indicating that her daughter had a history of regrettably unstable behavior.

Tasting her iced coffee, Carol was delighted to find that it packed a considerable caffeine jolt. "I suppose the shock of her husband's murder —" she began.

"Brin's death? Yes. But it was more than that." Iniga went on in a lower voice, "Leta is not able to have children. She had an inflammatory pelvic disease when she was younger. I'm afraid she was a little . . . wild."

She paused, then continued, "The hope was, naturally, that Brin, being a fertility specialist, could help her. They both wanted children very much, of course. I think the disappointment has quite turned her mind."

Iniga tapped the side of the thermal jug with one pink-varnished nail. "Do you have children, Inspector?"

"I have a son."

"A son?" Iniga seemed surprised. "How old is he?"

"A teenager — just."

"Conrad would have been entering his teens now, had he lived."

Carol broke the silence that followed this statement by asking, "This overdose — who found your daughter?"

"Found? No one found her. She called here, and her father could tell, just on the phone, that something was wrong. Perry rushed around to the penthouse and found Leta confused and irrational. Immediately, he contacted Naomi."

"Had your daughter left a note?"

"There was no note. Perry would have mentioned it, if there had been."

Carol asked, "Do you think this was a serious suicide attempt?"

"Leta didn't know what she was doing," said Iniga, her tone assured. "She was delusional. I've seen her this way before, on too many occasions. She can be frenzied, vicious."

In different circumstances, Carol would have been amused by the meaningful look that accompanied this statement. Obediently, Carol took the cue. "Are you saying that Leta might be capable of violence?"

Iniga gave a delicate gesture of acceptance. "As her mother, I don't want to even contemplate such a thing, but in all honesty, I have to say that it could be possible."

"Do you believe her capable of bludgeoning her husband, then setting the clinic on fire?

A shadow of distaste crossed Iniga's face, apparently a reaction to the bluntness of Carol's question.

"I don't want to believe it," she said, "but Perry's beside himself with worry, because *he's* convinced there's a real possibility that she had a psychotic episode and doesn't remember what she did."

How convenient, thought Carol, *and how remarkable that Leta Halstead stood in my office and obliquely suggested her parents might be suspects in her husband's murder.*

"You have no evidence?"

"No evidence, Inspector." Iniga spread her hands, palms up. The gesture was neatly performed, almost as though she had practiced it for this very occasion. "Just the obvious anxiety and dread that it might be so."

"And what would be her motive?"

Iniga grimaced. "Leta's so disturbed . . ."

"Even if that's true, there's some reason, something that triggers the violence."

"I can't think of anything specific."

"What sort of car does your daughter drive?"

Taken aback at this change of subject, Iniga said, "Car? Why, it's a white BMW. Why do you want to know?"

Thinking of the name on the back of the photograph of Brin Halstead, Carol said, "Does the name *Keith* mean anything to you?"

"Really, I can't see . . . Keith?" She frowned. "Oh, yes, I remember. He was a friend of Leta's from her teens." She smoothed one eyebrow with little brushing motions. "He's gay, I believe."

"You don't know his full name?"

"I've no idea."

Carol said, "It's been suggested to us that your son-in-law had disappointed you and your husband in some way."

"That's ridiculous. Frankly, he was close to a saint, the things he put up with from Leta." She gave a vexed sigh. "No doubt it was she who told you that."

"He was in severe financial trouble, perhaps to the point of losing the clinic."

"It was a temporary embarrassment, only. The cost of establishing world-class laboratories and keeping up with the most up-to-date equipment is considerable."

"You loaned him money."

"I gave him a gift. He was part of the family."

"Could Dr. Halstead have had a gambling problem?"

"That's ridiculous."

"Or blackmail. That would explain these unaccounted for withdrawals."

A strange expression flickered across Iniga Alaric's face, but all she said was, "This is rather in the realm of fiction, Inspector Ashton, not reality." She made a few fussy movements, as though preparing to leave. "Now, if there's nothing else . . ."

"We interviewed Faye Pickerson yesterday." Carol was casual.

Iniga turned her head quickly. "Indeed?"

"She spoke very highly of your kindness."

"A very healthy young woman." Iniga didn't sound approving, but cautious.

"I imagine you're awaiting the birth with great anticipation."

Obviously distrustful of Carol's sunny tone, Iniga Alaric said, "I appreciate your interest, Inspector, but I can't imagine that this has anything at all to do with Brin's murder."

"I was wondering if you'd considered DNA testing of the fetus."

Iniga's face flushed. "And why would we? It was Brin's last gift to us — our new son. There's no point in any tests, as we know exactly what they will show."

Assuming a look of mild surprise, Carol said, "But I understand a DNA test *has* been carried out."

Iniga's jaw dropped a little, then she recovered. "You must be mistaken."

"It was, I'm told, at your daughter's instigation."

Getting to her feet, Iniga said, her voice icy, "You are mistaken. The idea of a DNA test is ludicrous. All it would show is that Faye Pickerson will give birth to my husband's child, conceived in the laboratory using a donor egg and Perry's sperm."

A soft cough startled them both. The woman in black stood at attention, her hands clasped in front of her. "I'm sorry to interrupt, but Mr. Alaric would like to see Inspector Ashton before she leaves."

"The Inspector will go with you now, Janet. I don't believe we have anything more to discuss."

Carol followed Janet up the sweeping stairs that she had admired on the way to the conservatory, and into a study so aggressively masculine that she wanted to smile. Everywhere there was leather and dark polished wood. Mounted game fish were displayed on the walls, and there were several framed engravings of different stages of an English fox hunt. Carol noticed with distaste that the last showed the fox being torn to pieces by the hounds.

She glanced at the photographs. The blown-up images were of Perry Alaric, his soft body clad in the appropriate outfit, on safari, standing by a strung-up shark, and posing on a golf course with a trio of famous professional golfers.

Alaric's drooping eyelids and spongy face gave him an innocuous, innocent air, but Carol knew him to be a formidable businessman, whose ruthlessness was well known in the building industry. It was a surprise to see him out of a business suit. He was wearing old slacks and a faded sports shirt.

He shook hands with her and indicated a burgundy leather chair that turned out to be as uncomfortable as it looked. "Thank you, Inspector Ashton, for making time to see me. Iniga, I know, has told you about poor Leta."

"Yes, she has."

"I say this in confidence, but I fear, I very much fear, that Leta may have had something to do with Brin's death. She seems to be burning with the most extraordinary anger, Inspector, and when I asked her what was wrong, she —" He broke off, looking embarrassed, cleared his throat, and went on "Leta physically attacked me."

"Your wife tells me that Naomi Reed has admitted your daughter for treatment after what may have been a suicide attempt."

He nodded slowly. "I wanted to talk privately to you because, frankly, I'd like to know if you have any evidence that might incriminate my daughter."

Before she could speak, he put up a large, soft hand. "Don't worry, Inspector, I'm not asking for any specific details, just the general trend of your thinking. I'd like to be prepared for the worst, as it were. And I must assure you that if my daughter is guilty, although she'll have the best legal representation money can buy, that I don't intend for her to escape paying for her actions."

"This is very early in the inquiry," said Carol, both intrigued and outraged that Alaric should expect that she would openly discuss the conduct of the investigation with him.

"I've read somewhere," said Perry Alaric, "that the first forty-eight hours of an investigation are the vital ones, where most arrests are made. It's been more than four days now, so I do think it's reasonable to ask about the progress of the case. My son-in-law is dead, and my daughter may be responsible."

"I can't discuss the investigation with you, Mr. Alaric."

He seemed affronted by Carol's refusal to co-operate. "I don't think you understand, Inspector. This will be quite off the record."

Carol was losing patience. "Off the record or on the record, it makes no difference. I will not discuss my investigation with you."

"I see. And would it change your attitude if I told you I know the commissioner very well?"

She had pleasure in saying, "It would make no difference at all."

The Naomi Reed Clinic was as Carol remembered it. The building, which looked like a substantial mansion, rather than a hospital for the treatment of emotional and mental disorders, was surrounded by beautiful grounds, with rolling lawns and beds of bright flowers. The soothing sound of falling water came from the fountain at the entrance.

Anne Newsome threw her head back and regarded the sandstone facade. "If you've got to be mad, it helps to have money," she said.

Inside, they were taken immediately to Naomi Reed's office. Dressed in a starched white coat, her hair in an impeccable chignon, she radiated crisp professionalism. She came from behind her sleek desk to shake their hands. "Inspector Ashton, how very nice to see you again." She smiled at Anne Newsome. "And I believe we've met once before."

Carol was impressed: It had been three or four years, and Anne had been in the background during the interview.

"When we spoke on the phone," said Carol, "you said that Leta Halstead would be pleased to see me."

"Please sit," said the doctor. When they were settled on the peach-upholstered chairs, she went on, "I believe it's in Leta's best interests to talk with you." She glanced at Anne's open notebook and frowned slightly.

"Best interests medically, or personally?" asked Carol, with a half smile.

"Both."

"When I spoke to her mother this morning, she implied that Leta was too unstable to see anyone."

Naomi Reed's mouth tightened. "I'm afraid Iniga may have exaggerated the situation."

"What is the situation?" asked Carol.

"It's not breaking any medical confidences to tell you the obvious. Leta is grieving the violent death of her husband. She's frightened and upset."

"Did she attempt suicide?"

Without hesitation the doctor said, "No." She gave a grim little smile. "Perhaps I'll amend that to say, in my professional opinion, Leta was confused and took one too many sleeping pills." She looked expectantly at Carol, as though encouraging the next question.

It was like a dance around the truth, Carol thought. Naomi Reed obviously wanted to tell her more than she felt she could ethically, so Carol must ask the right questions and evaluate the answers to see what was hidden in them.

"Iniga Alaric implied that Leta had a history of mental instability."

"Unhappiness can lead one to self-destructive behavior." Dr. Reed raised her eyebrows. "That's just a general observation."

Carol's lips twitched. "Of course."

"Leta has not been admitted as a patient. She's chosen to stay here for a few days to get her thoughts together. As you'll understand, her life has been turned upside down."

"I was told this morning that Leta was delusional, and that she physically attacked her father."

"I can only repeat that I saw no need to admit her as a patient."

"If I were to describe Leta Halstead as psychotic . . . ?"

"You would be mistaken, Inspector."

"Off the record," said Carol, "both Iniga and Perry Alaric have made it clear that they believe that Leta is very likely to be guilty of her husband's murder."

"The motives people have for saying things are many," said Naomi Reed briskly, "and I think all strong statements should be viewed in that light."

The doctor stood, making it clear the interview was over.

Following the attendant leading them to Leta Halstead's room, Anne said to Carol, "I'd say Dr. Reed thinks the Alarics are trying to set up Leta for the murder by saying their daughter's mad, bad, and dangerous to know."

"Admirably succinct," said Carol. "And I think I know why."

CHAPTER FIFTEEN

"I'm sorry. I behaved badly last time we met. I felt . . . besieged." Taking a cigarette, Leta tapped it rapidly on the pack, then put it in her mouth. She looked around, searching for a light. Anne handed her matches from the table.

"Thanks." Leta took a deep breath, then let out a stream of smoke. "That's good. Naomi says I should stop, but I said to her, if I can't smoke in these circumstances, when can I?"

"When indeed," said Carol.

Leta shot her a scornful look. "If you only knew!"

"Perhaps I do."

The room was pastel shades — the walls, carpet, and furniture blended in a soothing harmony. Carol moved to the window. Looking out, she could see a slope of smooth grass and a stand of gum trees. A couple strolled, deep in conversation. Carol wondered if the two were patient and visitor. She watched them closely, trying to gain a hint of their roles. *Other people's lives,* she thought, suddenly feeling like a voyeur. She turned back to the room when Leta spoke.

"It's not just Brin's death. It's all these bloody pregnant women." She gave an angry laugh. "I'm just envious, of course."

Leta seemed unable to keep still. Arms folded, she paced around the room, at intervals sucking hard on the cigarette. Her dark hair was tousled, and she looked very young in faded jeans and an oversize white top.

"I have some questions," said Carol, "and I'm afraid a murder investigation means that I have to disregard good taste and propriety."

Leta stopped to light another cigarette from the butt of the one she'd been smoking. "You intrigue me, Inspector." Her glanced flicked to Anne, who had her notebook open and a pen at the ready. "Whatever could you be going to ask?"

"Did your husband have samples of his sperm frozen?"

Leta let her hands drop. After a moment she said, "Not to my knowledge. Brin was always ready and able to provide fresh samples. I can't imagine it occurred to him to freeze any. Why would he? He wasn't going anywhere, or so he thought."

"Do *you* have eggs frozen?"

Leta finished lighting the second cigarette. She took a reflective puff before saying, "With my mother around to tell everyone, it's no secret that I can't conceive, so yes, Brin harvested eggs from me, but it wasn't any use. I've had three IVF procedures, but not one of them has worked."

"Did your husband ever discuss cloning with you?"

"Brin and I rarely discussed anything much. Frankly, he didn't consider me particularly bright."

"Does that mean you didn't discuss cloning?"

"How persistent you are, Inspector Ashton. We didn't discuss cloning of anyone, or anything." She looked over at Anne. "I hope you've got that down."

Leta resumed her pacing, then stopped in front of Carol to say, "My mother called me this morning. She said that she thought it very unwise for me to speak to the police, and especially to you, Inspector. She said to ask Naomi to say I was too sick to be interviewed."

Carol didn't respond. Leta gave her a faint smile and said, "Why would that be?"

"You'll have to ask your mother."

Leta inspected the end of her cigarette. "Do you remember I said I came from a family of liars?"

"I remember."

"My mother is telling everyone I'm mad. Did you know that?" She gave a short laugh. "Of course you do. The idea is to blame me for Brin's murder. 'Poor Leta,' my parents will cry, 'she didn't know what she was doing.'"

"Are you saying your mother is lying?"

Leta shrugged. "Perhaps she believes it. Anyway,

she thinks she's bringing a lawyer here this afternoon so I can sign a document giving her power of attorney over my affairs."

"Are you going to sign it?"

"I'll refuse to see any lawyer, and I won't see my parents, or even speak with them, for that matter. My mother is insisting that it's for my own good, that I should sign everything over to her until I get better, although she and I both know she'll never believe that day has come."

"Your husband left a will."

"Yes, one of the few responsible things Brin did." She made a face at Carol. "Everything comes to me. It gives me a motive, I suppose, though basically what I've inherited is mostly debts."

"Would you give us permission to go through your husband's private papers? We'd also like to search your penthouse."

Carol expected a refusal and was resigned to getting a search warrant, but Leta said, "Sure. I haven't any objection."

Carol handed her the photograph of Brin Halstead that Iniga Alaric had given to her the day of the first interview. "There's a name on the back."

Leta turned it over. "Yes, Keith. Keith Shales, actually. I've known him for years. He's a photographer in Darlinghurst, and I used to see him a lot. Brin liked him, I thought, but then I realized that it was what Brin thought Keith could do for him that was the attraction."

"Which was?"

"Keith's gay. Since Brin couldn't advertise some of the things the Halstead Clinic was offering, he used Keith to get the word out in the gay community.

Once word of mouth had worked, Brin didn't need Keith, so he dumped him."

"And you didn't continue to see him?"

A shrug. "I could have, but after a while, I didn't bother."

Although she was thinking how selfish and self-absorbed Leta was, Carol maintained an expression of polite inquiry. "Do you have an address for Keith Shales?"

"It's in the book. He's a well-known photographer."

"I gather one of the services the clinic was offering that couldn't be advertised was cloning."

"Was it? I didn't pay much attention."

"That surprises me," said Carol. "I've been told you arranged for a DNA profile of the child Faye Pickerson is carrying."

"That's a lie," said Leta flatly.

"So you didn't show anyone evidence that the baby was the clone of your brother, Conrad?"

"Of course I didn't, and you won't find records in any testing lab that proves I did."

"Faye Pickerson says that you've been to visit her quite often."

"Why wouldn't I? She's a surrogate for my father — she's going to have his child."

"With a donor egg?"

"With a donor egg from some anonymous woman." With an unpleasant smile, she added, "A perfectly normal conception, if you like your sex in a glass dish. I'm sure my father would have preferred a more conventional method, but there you are."

Carol put out her hand for the photograph, which Leta still held. Instead of passing it back, Leta looked pensively at the image of her husband. "This is a good likeness of Brin. He was sexy. Sexy and slick as hell. And he liked to make me jealous. It used to amuse him when he provoked me and I lost it and yelled at him."

"Did you have reason to be jealous?"

"I thought I did."

Carol said, "You were following him the night he died. You were seen driving near the clinic." It was merely an educated guess, but Carol delivered it as an incontrovertible fact.

"Who saw me?" Making an exasperated sound, Leta flicked the photo onto the couch near where Anne sat. "Oh, it doesn't matter. When Brin came home he was in a shitty mood."

"This was around seven-thirty?"

"Something like that."

"How long does it take to drive from the clinic to your place?"

She made a vague gesture. "I don't know — a few minutes."

"And what happened after your husband got home?"

"Nothing much."

"Were there any calls while he was there?"

Leta's hesitation was only momentary. "No, none."

"Why did you follow him when he left?"

"He got himself something to eat — I was watching television — then he came in and picked a fight."

"About what?"

"The usual stuff. I was no fun anymore, I should have a hot meal on the table when he came home, etcetera, etcetera. I told him to get lost, and he grabbed his car keys and stormed out of the place. I was sure he'd engineered it so he could get out to meet some new girlfriend."

She looked at Carol with a trace of defiance. "I had good reason to think so, you know. He had girlfriends before, usually straight out of school — kids he could impress. And he didn't stop there. I always suspected he put the hard word on some of his clients. He really was a bit of a bastard, but so bloody charming you could almost forgive him anything."

Extinguishing her cigarette with a vicious stabbing action, she said sardonically, "It's at this point I say I didn't kill him. That's what they do in movies. The beautiful widow denies everything."

Quite a performance, Carol thought. She saw Anne turn a page, careful not to make a distracting noise.

Carol said, "And when you followed him on Wednesday night . . . ?"

"He went to Gilda's place. She's got a flat in Potts Point. I parked in the street and sat and thought what a creep Brin was, running to her to complain about me."

Before Carol could respond, Leta added derisively, "No, I didn't think he was having an affair with her. Hell, *I'm* almost too old for him."

Leta picked up the cigarette pack. "He was there for ages and I got bored and I'd forgotten my smokes, so I started to drive off, but just as I did, I saw Brin come out and get in his car. So I did a quick U-turn — almost flattened some old woman walking her poodle — and took off after him. Didn't catch him up, but I could see his car in the distance, and I realized he was going to the clinic. When I got there, I saw his BMW turning into the lane, so I drove around the block a few times, deciding what to do."

"And what did you do?"

"It's funny when I think of it now, but I needed to go to the bathroom, and I really wanted a cigarette, so I thought, to hell with it, and went home."

As Carol and Anne were leaving the building, Carol stopped by the fountain to speak to a stocky woman hurrying toward the entrance. "Ms. Milton? May I have a word with you?"

Gilda Milton, obviously discomfited, halted. "Inspector Ashton." She blinked her pale eyes, collecting herself, then said briskly, "I'm afraid I'm in rather a hurry."

"This is Detective Constable Newsome," Carol said.

Gilda barely glanced at Anne. "I'm sure. Now —"

"I thought you might still be helping Sergeant Bourke at the clinic."

"He didn't need me, and I had other work to do."

"You're visiting Leta Halstead?"

Plainly reluctant, Gilda replied, "Why, yes."

"I didn't realize you were friends." Carol's tone was innocent, as though making a casual observation.

"We're not. That is, we're not exactly friends."

Carol looked encouraging.

Regaining her self-possession, Gilda said, "As Dr.

Halstead's personal assistant, I'm conversant with the day-to-day running of the clinic. I did think that Mrs. Halstead would appreciate being kept abreast of what is happening."

"Surely Dr. Vail could do that?"

For a moment her face showed amusement. "I'm afraid Bill Vail and Leta don't get on very well, so you might look upon me as a go-between in the situation."

"You said you were home alone the night Dr. Halstead died."

"Yes." Gilda watched Carol warily.

"But you failed to mention that Dr. Halstead visited you that evening."

"You're mistaken. He didn't."

"Leta Halstead says he did. After an argument, she followed her husband after he left their place. She says he drove straight to you."

"And you believe Leta?"

"I'm inclined to, yes."

Anne took out her notebook. Flicking a few pages, she said, "I believe we may have a corroborative witness."

Nice work, thought Carol.

There was a pause while Gilda obviously debated how to respond. Then she said, "All right, he did call in. Brin was furious with Leta, and he needed somewhere to go and blow off steam. He calmed down after a while, and he left."

"Why didn't you mention this previously?"

"I didn't want to make trouble for Leta, and I didn't want to get involved. Simple as that. Besides, it wasn't going to be of any help to you to know about it."

"I would like to have been the judge of that."

Bristling at Carol's cool tone, Gilda said, "Okay, so I'll make a written statement. It won't do you any good, but it'll satisfy the legalities, I suppose."

Carol said, "Leta Halstead was just driving away when her husband came out. I was wondering if it might be possible that *two* people got into his car."

"What are you implying? That *I* left with Brin? I'm not going to waste time talking about anything so ludicrous. I'm sorry, but I must go."

Watching her ample form disappearing into the building, Carol said, "Tell Maureen to hurry up with the financial backgrounds on everyone, especially Gilda Milton, and to check Australia-wide for property or business investments."

"You're considering that Gilda Milton could be a blackmailer?"

"I think we can narrow it down to someone who was in a position to get firm evidence to convince Halstead he had to pay through the nose. That almost certainly means a person at the clinic, and the best bets, I'd say, are Bill Vail, Gilda Milton, Elaine Kaynes, and maybe Tom Lorant."

"And Ursula Vail?"

"She has a more personal resentment, perhaps hatred, toward Halstead."

"So murder, not mere blackmail, would be the way she'd go?" said Anne, grinning.

"Perhaps," said Carol, a vivid image of Ursula Vail wielding a gardening implement rising in her mind. The picture her imagination painted had the woman raising a shovel to deliver the coup de grâce to Brin

Halstead, but she wondered if Ursula, in reality, had something like a crowbar in her gardening shed.

When they got to the car, Carol ticked off Anne's jobs. "I want you to check the Halstead personal telephone records for the days up to his death, especially for Wednesday evening, as well as for the days following. In fact, pull the telephone records on the Vails and the Alarics as well."

"What about the poodle woman?" said Anne. "I mean the one Leta said she nearly squashed when she was doing a u-ey. She might have seen something."

"If someone's available, okay. But I want you to stay on the important stuff, like whether Ursula Vail is telling the truth about her whereabouts on Wednesday evening, and if Iniga and Perry Alaric were really enjoying each other's company when their son-in-law was dying."

Pulling smoothly out into the traffic, Anne said, "Why do you think Leta was really visiting Faye? She doesn't seem to like her parents much, so why would she bother?"

Carol remembered Noelle Winthall saying scornfully that Leta was worried about her inheritance, but perhaps it was more than that. "Anne, find out if Leta stopped going to see Faye Pickerson, say three or four weeks ago."

"When she found out it was a clone."

"*If* she found out the baby was a clone."

"This whole cloning thing," said Anne, adroitly avoiding a vehicle making a surprise turn, "is really weird, isn't it? Did you see the article by Noelle Winthall in the paper this morning?"

"I didn't get much past the front page, especially

the coverage of the Halstead murder. It's obvious someone in the know is leaking information."

Anne glanced over at her. "You think it's from us?"

"It's possible. Just keep an eye out, Anne."

"On anyone in particular?"

"I don't want to accuse someone and then be wrong." Carol felt betrayed that someone she worked with might be collecting money under the table for information. To change the subject, she said, "So what was in Noelle Winthall's cloning article?"

Anne was filled with gee-whiz enthusiasm. "It's totally off-the-planet stuff. Did you know that they can make multiple clones of animals, and soon humans, so that you can order twins, or triplets, or however many you want, and every one will be exactly the same? Then you can choose to have one implanted in you, or in a surrogate mother, and the others can be frozen to be used later on."

"I imagine that means that you could have identical twins in a family, but one might be, say, twenty, and the other ten?"

"Awful, isn't it?" said Anne with every evidence of enjoyment. "Or you could just have one of the babies and keep the others frozen as little clumps of cells that could be activated and used as replacements if the first one died somewhere along the line. And there's even creepier stuff than that. For instance, you could use a clone to provide organs for trans- plants, since there'd be no rejection problem. Sort of like a spare-parts person. Gross, eh?"

Entering into the spirit of the conversation, Carol said, "What if you had a clone of yourself and brought it up? I suppose you'd understand the kid better than anyone else could."

"But they wouldn't be the same as you, would they?" said Anne. "I mean, the world they grew up in, what happened to them at school — all of that would be different."

"Well, having your twin as a parent would be different, I give you that," said Carol.

Anne shook her head. "You know, the thing that really got to me was the church guy who actually said a clone couldn't have a soul, so he or she couldn't go to heaven."

"Or hell," said Carol.

CHAPTER SIXTEEN

"I've got to leave for a job in twenty minutes," said Keith Shales. His face reminded Carol of one of the sadder looking hounds, but his voice was cheerful.

Carol looked around his little studio, crammed with photographic gear and lights. "I'll be quick. You knew Brin Halstead?"

He looked resigned. "Yes, I was wondering when you'd get around to me. Actually, it was Leta I knew best. Believe it or not, we went to school together, and we kept in touch."

"And through her you met Brin Halstead."

He rubbed at his chin. "I've an impeccable alibi, Inspector Ashton, or I wouldn't say this, but Brin deserved all he got. He was past due, in my book. A real bastard who should have been eliminated long ago."

"It's delightful to find someone so forthright," said Carol, smiling.

He grinned in turn. "I tell it like I see it. I suppose I'm still angry because he sucked me in with all the wonderful things he was going to do for gays and lesbians. A new world dawning, he said, where you don't have to fight for years to adopt a child, where nobody can claim custody of your kid because genetically it's yours and no one else's."

"He was talking cloning."

Shales nodded, his heavy jowls shaking. "He was talking cloning. And I still believe he had the skill to do it. That wasn't what turned me against the fucker."

"No doubt you'll tell me."

He laughed. "No doubt I will. Nobody ever called me a shrinking violet."

He began to collect photographic equipment as he went on. "The fact is, although it took a while, I began to see what Brin Halstead really was. He could charm the pants off anybody, but underneath, he didn't give shit about anyone's feelings or rights. To himself, he was a god, playing with people's lives."

"A sociopath?"

"You can put a label on anyone, Inspector. I'd just say Brin Halstead was evil. There are so many couples desperate to have children, and that amused him, I came to understand. He liked people to want something from him so he could give or withhold, according to his whim of the moment. And, of course, he screwed Leta royally."

"You don't mean literally, I take it?"

"I mean both. But mainly, he really messed with her mind. She wanted a baby. Did Leta tell you that?"

"Yes." Carol watched his hands as he slotted items into bags. Shales's movements were quick and precise, and he hardly hesitated in his selections. "She told me that all the IVF attempts had failed."

"You know how it works, I suppose. The woman's given fertility drugs, and these encourage multiple eggs to form in the ovaries. Then the eggs are extracted. Some are used straightaway, but most of them are frozen for later."

"And?"

"And after Leta's first couple of failures, Brin told her that she'd never be pregnant and that he was distributing her eggs at random, to anyone who he fancied might like a child with, as he so delicately put it, special emotional needs. Of course, all the patient was told was it was a donor egg from a healthy young woman."

Carol tried to imagine how it would feel to be betrayed by someone who was not only a doctor, sworn to ethical standards, but also a marriage partner. "How did Leta react?"

His sincere hound's face creased with sympathy. "When Leta told me about it, she was terribly upset, but then she changed and went into complete denial, saying that she knew Brin was joking, that he'd never do such a thing. When I insisted that he would, she broke off our friendship." He checked his watch. "Sorry, I've got to go."

180

"One thing," said Carol, as he slung bags of equipment over his shoulders. "Do you think there's any possibility she's right? However cruel it was, that he was just joking?"

"I'm sure he did just what he said." He ushered her out the door and locked it behind them. "And worse."

"You've got a leak," said Madeline, her voice singing down the electronic connections to Carol's mobile phone, "and I just happen to have a name."

"If you're willing to tell me a name, I imagine it means the leaking is going to the opposition, not to you."

"How cynical you are, Carol, but as it happens, you're right. And fortunately for you, someone at the paper owes me a favor, and I called it in. I was sworn to secrecy, but for you . . ."

"Who is it?" asked Carol. "And please, Madeline, don't make me jump through hoops for this."

"As if I would, although I like the picture it makes. Perhaps dinner?"

"Perhaps."

"It's one Rafe Janach, and he's pretty pricey, I hear. Are you surprised?"

"Not so surprised," Carol said.

Maureen Oatland was waiting for Carol when she got back to her office. "Two for the price of one," she said, depositing a pile of papers on Carol's desk.

"I believe the dear doctor may have had two blackmailers, not one."

Carol looked at the heaped papers without enthusiasm. "How about you give me a summary?"

"Done." Maureen plopped down in the chair in front of the desk. "Gilda Milton has recently paid cash for a very spiffy unit on the Gold Coast, plus some substantial dabbling in the stock market that can't possibly be supported by her income — and she hasn't inherited from a rich uncle, either. And Elaine Kaynes, though not quite on that level, has just bought a house for cash in Chippendale."

"Two blackmailers operating at the same time with the same victim?" said Carol. "It would be a first for me, if it's so."

"Why the same victim?" said Maureen. "Hell, everyone's got secrets. Who knows? Maybe Gilda shakes down Halstead, while Elaine has slimmer pickings with Vail."

"Elaine's windfall could be part of the Daris settlement. Tom Lorant says she blew the whistle that alerted the parents."

"Could be," said Maureen, clearly disappointed at the prospect.

"And Halstead's will?"

"His will's as simple as they come. He leaves absolutely everything to his wife — money, shares, patents, the lot."

"How many patents does he hold?"

Maureen grinned. "Several, but I know it's the cloning one you're after, so don't bother to hide it. Halstead has an application in for a patent using a new method. I was never very good at biology in school. But I was given a rundown from the patent

182

lawyer, so I've got the general picture. Halstead's method is very like previous ones, but the chemical agent used to start the cloning process is different. Whatever — if it works, it could be worth billions."

"So Leta will be a very rich widow."

"Not if she murdered him, she won't," said Maureen. "It's a bitch, isn't it, the way they won't let you inherit from your nearest and dearest if you bump them off?"

The phone rang while Maureen, still chuckling, was leaving the office.

"Have you eaten today?" asked Sybil.

Carol smiled. "Maureen Oatland has much junk food on her desk. I grazed a little each time I passed by."

"Then how about dinner?"

"Darling, I can't. As it is, I'll have to ask my long-suffering neighbor to feed Sinker yet again."

Carol looked up to see Bourke at the door, a folder under his arm. "Sorry, I have to go."

Sybil said, "Do I have to wait until the case is over?"

"It won't be long now."

Carol said these words with absolute conviction. Each case had a rhythm and a pattern. With this one she could sense things gathering, coalescing. The picture wasn't clear yet, but the pieces, she knew, would soon slide together to show the intricate designs of wants and needs, of motives and opportunities.

Carol said good-bye and looked at Bourke. "How did it go?"

"At the clinic, nothing new. The client files in the office were largely destroyed in the fire, and I can't make head or tail of the lab notes that survived. Even so, Dr. Vail twittered every time I looked at anything he thought might refer to a celebrity client."

"There were several mentioned on the front page this morning."

"Bill Vail blames us."

"He may be right," said Carol.

Bourke raised his eyebrows. "Who?"

"Madeline says Janach."

A look of distaste crossed his face. "Jesus. Have you said anything yet?"

"Not yet."

Bourke put his folder on her desk and slumped into a chair, stretching out his long legs. "Where was I? I gave up at the clinic and took Ferguson with me to give the Halstead penthouse a quick going-over. Sadly, we found no murder weapon. We'd only been there half an hour or so when Iniga Alaric came through the door. She said Gilda Milton had told her Leta had given us permission and had arranged for security to let us in, but I could see she wasn't confident we could be trusted not to smash some valuable knickknack."

"So she stayed?"

"Short of carrying her out bodily, there was no way to get rid of her." He tilted his head thoughtfully. "You know, I almost felt she wanted us to find the contract between Halstead and Noelle Winthall. She made a point of showing us Brin Halstead's desk in the den, saying he often kept documents there."

Bourke passed the folder over the desk to Carol. "Here it is. I'll get a legal opinion, if you like, but even to me it looks like Noelle got screwed. She was to do all the work of writing and Halstead was to get the glory and two-thirds of the money."

Carol hid a yawn. "Come on," said Bourke. "Want to share a hamburger with me at Greasy Joe's?"

"That's too alluring an invitation to turn down. And then we pay a visit to Elaine Kaynes."

As they passed Anne she was putting down her phone. "You were right," she said to Carol. "Leta Halstead stopped calling in to see Faye about a month ago. Thelma Pickerson said she was quite pleased when it happened. She said she thought Leta was unbalanced — she used rather more colorful language — and she'd wondered if one day Leta might hurt Faye and the baby."

"I didn't blackmail anybody!" Elaine Kaynes was flushed. Her blue eyes glinting, she said, "Everything was aboveboard."

Bourke looked down at the sheet he held. "You paid cash for a house in Chippendale."

"So? I got money for the Daris case." She added quickly, "I was paid, very generously, to be an expert witness. That's why the insurance company settled before the trial really got underway. They knew I'd tell the truth."

Carol said, "Payment as an expert witness hardly seems enough to buy a house. Where did the rest of the money come from?"

"It's only a tiny place." Elaine made an awkward gesture. "You know, quite small. I'm renting it out, but one day I hope to move there myself."

"You had a source of income other than your salary."

Carol's words seemed to deflate Elaine. Her shoulders drooped and she looked at the floor. "Gilda," she said.

"Gilda Milton?"

She nodded slowly. "Gilda paid me for information. I mean, as head of the nursing staff, I knew what was going on."

Carol gave a grim smile. "The IVF irregularities that the media has been referring to?"

"Yes, that, but other things too. Gilda paid me for names and addresses. And anything to do with Leta Halstead."

CHAPTER SEVENTEEN

Although it was very early when Carol and Bourke walked in together, Anne was already hard at work. Carol was envious: Although Anne could not have had much sleep, she was as bubbly and energetic as usual, bounding into Carol's office with a smile.

"I can give you a quick report on almost everything you asked for," Anne said. "First, the Vails. I asked the local cops to nose around, but finding corroboration for their movements on Wednesday is going to be hard."

"Second," she said with more enthusiasm, "the Halstead phone records." She passed Carol a sheet. "See the two calls I've highlighted? At seven-twenty there's one from the Alaric house that lasts five minutes. Then at two minutes to eight there's a call from the Halstead penthouse back to the Alarics. It only lasts forty seconds."

"I can tell from your expression you have more," said Carol, repressing an indulgent smile.

"I spoke to Janet, the Alarics' housekeeper, first thing this morning."

"Hell, it must have been at dawn!"

"Thereabouts," said Anne with satisfaction. "Fortunately, she gets up early. She took the call made from the Halstead penthouse just before eight on Wednesday night. It was Leta Halstead, and Janet said she sounded almost hysterical. She wanted to speak to her father, urgently, but Janet said she'd just seen him go out, so Leta had missed him."

"Janet said before that Iniga and Perry Alaric were in all night."

"I pointed that out," said Anne. "She got all frosty on me and said that there was such a thing as loyalty, and since it was impossible that Mr. Alaric had anything to do with the murder, she thought it quite a reasonable request when he suggested she forget that he'd been out."

"We need a statement."

"I'll get it today. There is something more you should know. Janet said that Leta Halstead has checked herself out of the hospital and is expected at the Alaric house any moment now."

Carol felt a kick of excitement. "Tell Mark to

meet me at his car," she said. "We have two urgent calls to make."

"The early bird gets the worm," said Bourke. He knocked sharply on the door of Gilda Milton's apartment.

She opened it, frowning, a mug of coffee in one hand. "What is it?"

"It's difficult to hide large sums of money, isn't it?" said Carol pleasantly.

Gilda Milton stepped back from the door, her face pasty white. "I don't know what you mean." She put the mug down on the nearest table, heedless of the damage the heat might cause.

"I think you do," said Bourke. He followed Carol inside and shut the door behind them. Picking up her discarded coffee, he walked toward the kitchen alcove to place it on the bench beside a plate holding a piece of half-eaten toast. "You've been blackmailing Brin Halstead for some time."

"That's not true." Gilda licked her lips. "Brin loaned me money, but he didn't want anyone to know." In a stronger voice she added, "It was a private arrangement."

"I have a list of your recent investments," said Bourke. "Halstead was extraordinarily generous."

"And we've spoken with Elaine Kaynes," said Carol. "She was very helpful."

Gilda put a hand to her mouth. Carol could see the plump fingers shaking. "I'm asking you to leave."

Carol said, "We won't leave without you. We can arrest you, right now." She glanced at Bourke.

In formal tones, he began, "Gilda Maria Milton —"

"No! This can't be happening. It's a mistake." Gilda looked blindly around the apartment. "I need a lawyer."

"You do," said Carol. "And it would be more convenient for you to have legal representation before your arrest, I imagine."

Gilda looked from one to the other. "What is it you want from me?"

"The answer to some questions," said Bourke. "To start with, why were you visiting Leta Halstead at the hospital yesterday?"

"Mr. Alaric asked me to. Leta was refusing to take any calls, and he wanted me to give her a personal message. I was to tell her that he had everything under control and that she shouldn't tell the police anything at all." She gave a short laugh. "But I was a bit late, wasn't I?"

"When Brin Halstead came here last Wednesday evening, he wasn't just sounding off about his wife, was he?" said Carol.

"Brin said I'd blown it, telling Leta. When I said I didn't know what he was talking about, he told me I wouldn't get another cent from him. I asked him what he meant, but he swore at me — I thought he would hit me — and slammed out the door."

"The initial in the appointment book," said Carol. "That was meant to point suspicion at Ursula Vail, I presume?"

Gilda seemed embarrassed. "A bit amateur, I confess. I wrote in the U with a pencil, then partly erased it." Her expression changed to malice. "Of course Ursula's a bitch, and for all I know she *was* there and did murder Brin."

Hard-faced, Bourke said, "What dirt did you have on Halstead?"

Carol thought that Gilda wouldn't answer, but after a long silence, she said, "Brin was reckless, impulsive, and he lied to a lot of people, but he was confident he could bluff his way out of anything. The one thing he feared, though, was losing the support of his in-laws. I don't need to tell you how well-off the Alarics are, and Iniga in particular was very generous to Brin."

"And what did you have that would hurt that relationship?"

"Brin kept very detailed notes. He was so arrogant — he never thought he'd get caught. He used to joke that he had to keep track of what he was doing to whom, as if it were a game and he were keeping score. As head nurse, it wasn't hard for Elaine to get access, and I paid her to photocopy as many records as she could. She helped herself, too — got paid very well over the Daris case. Then she got greedy and wanted more money from me, so I had to raise it somehow to pay her."

"So it's Elaine Kaynes's fault that you started blackmailing?" said Bourke, not bothering to hide his scorn.

Gilda said to Carol, as though she'd understand, "When you're a woman and alone, you have to look after number one. No one else is going to do it for you. I wanted insurance for the time when Brin might try to get rid of me, trade me in for someone younger."

"Insurance was it?" said Bourke. "And when did the extortion start?"

"Brin could have made a fortune on his own, without worrying about the Alarics, but he was a spendthrift, a fool with money." Gilda's face burned with resentment. "Why shouldn't I want some for myself? Brin would have thrown it away, in any case."

"I'm losing patience," said Carol, her voice hard.

"All right." She took a deep breath. "He was using his own sperm with some patients, but saying it was from screened donors. I kept all the evidence, although I didn't try to do anything with it. But then Elaine gave me records that I could use. Leta Halstead had several tries with IVF, but they all failed. Brin had kept frozen eggs from her, and he started to use them without Leta's permission."

"You said Halstead could bluff his way out of most things," said Bourke. "Why not this time?"

"Two surrogates I know for sure have Leta's eggs — Cindy Farr and Faye Pickerson."

Carol could see where this was going. "Faye's carrying a baby that came from Leta's egg and Perry Alaric's sperm? There never was a clone of Conrad Alaric."

"Exactly," said Gilda.

"Jesus," said Bourke. "That's IVF incest, isn't it?"

Janet had brought refreshments to the living room, but no one had touched them. "I don't know where my parents are," said Leta. "I'm not their keeper."

Janet had been equally unhelpful. "I think they went out to breakfast somewhere. Maybe one of the hotels . . ."

Leta was all in white, but there was a smear of lipstick on the cuff of her long-sleeve shirt and a stain of what looked like coffee on the front.

Carol remained standing. "We just came from Gilda Milton, so we know all about the baby Faye Pickerson is carrying."

Leta fumbled for a cigarette. "God, it'll be a relief to tell you. I knew we could never keep it quiet."

She lit the cigarette with a shaking hand, then sat on the very edge of a chair, leaning forward to tap nonexistent ash into a ceramic ashtray. "I was worried that Faye might have been implanted with one of my eggs, and the thought that maybe my father's sperm had been used to fertilize it made me distraught, but I couldn't tell anyone, and I couldn't keep away from Faye. It was horrible. I wanted to persuade her to have an abortion, but I knew she wouldn't listen. The best I could do was hope she'd miscarry, but of course she didn't. Then, a month or so ago, I couldn't stand it any more, and I told Brin what I'd been thinking.

"I remember he was really nice. He could be, you know. He gave me a cuddle, and he said he'd show me something that would make it all okay. It was a DNA report, and it proved, he said, that Faye was carrying Conrad's clone. The match between the cells from the fetus and the frozen samples taken from Conrad when he died were identical. I wanted to believe him, and I was so relieved."

The extensive use of DNA profiling in law enforcement had made Carol familiar with the technique and its high reliability. The way the results were displayed in what looked like a supermarket bar code fascinated her.

"You showed the report to Noelle Winthall."

"Yes. She was so anxious to know if cloning could work. I know she suspected Brin had lied to her, but when she saw these results she was reassured."

Bourke said, "And when did you suspect the truth?"

Mashing her half-smoked cigarette, Leta said, "Elaine told me. Or, at least, she hinted so strongly that something was wrong that I confronted Brin."

Her mouth turned down in a bitter smile. "I bluffed him, which was a first. He always could see through me, but this time I fooled him. He thought Gilda had told me everything. He laughed so hard, I thought he'd cry. He said it would be our secret. That we could look at my new brother when he was born, and know that he was half mine. Brin was so sure I wouldn't tell my father. He was sure I wouldn't dare."

She got to her feet. "Sorry, I can't sit still." She picked up the teapot on the tray Janet had left, then put it down. "This is going to sound dramatic, but the next thing Brin said became his death warrant. He told me that he had plenty of my eggs and my father's sperm. That he had a mind to populate Sydney with our children. It amused him mightily. Our little secret, he said. Imagine when you see a kid, it could be yours. Will it be slim like you, or fat and soft like Perry?"

"But you did tell your father," Carol said.

"I told him everything last Wednesday morning, up in his study. I've never seen him look that way.

He listened, and he asked some questions. When he understood, his face went gray and he vomited, right there in front of me."

"What happened then?" Bourke prompted.

"My father said that Brin mustn't suspect that I'd told him anything. He would take care of it. He asked me to give him the spare set of keys to the clinic, saying he'd go there and destroy every specimen that was ours. Brin never went to the clinic at night, but I was to make sure he stayed with me at home."

"He called your penthouse on Wednesday night."

Leta sat down and began to shred the butts in the ashtray. "He telephoned Brin about half past seven, just to check that he was there. I heard Brin's side of the conversation, and it was ordinary. I think they made a lunch date for next week. But something must have made Brin suspicious, because after he put down the phone, he accused me of telling. I said no, of course.

"He was furious, raving at me that I'd spoiled everything. Then he left. The moment the door closed, I called my father to stop him from going to the clinic, but it was too late. I grabbed my keys and went after Brin. I remember thinking I should stop him somehow. He'd been held up at the traffic light on the corner, so I caught up with him and stayed behind him as he drove to Gilda's. Everything else is as I told you before. When I followed him to the clinic, I didn't know what to do. I drove around, feeling sick with fear, not able to decide whether to go in, or to call someone . . ."

"So you went home."

If Bourke's terse statement offended her, she

didn't show it. "There was nothing I could do. I thought they'd sort it out between them. I never imagined that Brin would die."

Janet came into the sitting room. "Inspector, there's an urgent call for you."

Carol picked up the phone with a sense of foreboding. Anne said, "We've got a hostage situation. It's at Faye Pickerson's place."

Carol found it strangely satisfying to have the sirens blaring. It gave a sense of speed, of righteous urgency. The quiet street had been closed off, police vehicles were parked haphazardly along the shoulders, and with more purpose as barriers, in front of the Pickerson house. Crowds of onlookers and the ubiquitous media trucks were already in evidence. Overhead a helicopter circled.

Iniga Alaric was sitting in the front of a patrol car, sobbing into a handkerchief. A young female officer sitting beside her offered futile words of comfort.

"She got out of the house and gave the alarm," said the officer in charge, indicating Iniga. "Her husband's inside with the daughter and mother. We're not sure if he's armed. We're just waiting for the hostage negotiator." He handed Carol a receiver. "In the meantime, we've got a phone link. He's been waiting for you to arrive."

"You've talked to Leta?" said Perry Alaric's heavy voice.

"Yes. We know everything."

"Not everything, Inspector. Come in. I won't hurt you."

When both Mark Bourke and the officer in charge protested, Carol showed them the subcompact Glock holstered in the small of her back. "But I doubt I'll need it," she said.

Perry Alaric ushered her in with courtesy. "I want you to understand," he said. He didn't appear to have a weapon, and he gave a tired smile when he noticed Carol checking him over.

Faye and Thelma were huddled together, eyes wide, on the sofa in the living room. He gestured for Carol to sit, then began in an almost bored voice, "Brin surprised me while I was splashing petrol around the laboratory. I wanted to destroy everything he valued. I'd already turned off the sprinkler system and opened the files with a tire iron, and, most important, I'd destroyed all the sperm and eggs I thought belonged to Leta and myself." He gave a small shrug. "Such little things. I washed them down the sink."

His casual demeanor changed as he went on, "That bastard walked in and screamed at me. What was I doing in his clinic? He smelled the petrol, saw what I was doing, and became insane with rage, incoherent. And that made me so savagely angry, because *I* was the wronged one, not him."

"Did he attack you?" said Carol.

"He moved toward me. Perhaps I thought he was going to hit me; I don't remember. He'd pulled out his wallet, and he was screaming something about how I'd cost him money."

Alaric hung his head. "It was all so quick. I

didn't think about it, I just snatched up the tire iron from the bench and hit him. He went down, but I couldn't stop. I could see my arm rising and falling and hear the noise of the blows, but somehow I was outside myself, watching it all happen."

He dusted his hands as though he had finished an important job. "There, it's over now. Everything is over. I'm sorry I frightened you, Faye. I knew everything was falling to pieces, and I had to get to you before it was too late."

Faye stared at him with blank dread. He said gently to her, "I'll pay for a late-term abortion and make it very worth your while."

"No abortion," said Thelma, who had rallied. She patted Faye's stomach. "This is your kid. He's got rights."

Carol saw a look of ineffable weariness come over Perry Alaric's face. "What is it? Do you want to keep the baby? Is it child support you're asking for?"

"Not child support," said Thelma, "though that would be nice. He's your son, isn't he?"

She paused, looked at Faye and Carol, then at last to Perry Alaric. "Your only son . . . and heir."

CHAPTER EIGHTEEN

Mark Bourke took a cold beer out of the cooler and surveyed the beach. "Great day," he said.

It was that, thought Carol. A cooling breeze blew off the water. The pale sand shimmered. The breaking waves were high enough to allow some spectacular surfing for the skilled, and some equally spectacular wipeouts for those who weren't.

Pat and Bourke reclined under one striped beach umbrella, Sybil and Carol under another. Sybil was slathered in sunburn cream, as her fair skin would redden with only a little exposure. She amused Carol by calling it "Getting some color," though, as Carol pointed out, bright pink was not the desired shade.

"Did you hear that Rafe Janach's resigned?" said Bourke. "It's a bit extreme, since he wasn't really PIC material."

He was referring to the Police Integrity Commission, established as a temporary measure to combat police corruption and showing no signs of ever being disbanded.

"Must have been the conversation you had with him, Carol," said Pat. "Mark tells me he came out of your office looking quite shaken."

Carol grimaced, thinking of the confrontation she'd had with Janach. "Unpleasant guy. I'm glad he's gone."

Little twin girls with red sand buckets and spades ran giggling down the beach to the edge of the water. Carol smiled at their concentration as they squatted together, inspecting the treasures thrown up by the tide.

She thought of the Halstead case and how it, like every investigation, had changed her. Her thoughts of family, of children, had altered in subtle ways. Her relationship with David was somehow different. And Sybil? Today Carol wasn't curious about the future. She was content to let the tides of life lap at her feet.

Pat, whose pregnancy was just starting to show, had been watching the twins, who were squealing with laughter as they splashed each other. "What's happening with the Alaric baby?" she asked.

"Iniga Alaric has decided he should be adopted," said Carol. "Thelma Pickerson put up a good fight on behalf of her daughter for custody, but lost."

"Dollar signs, that's what she saw," said Bourke. He lazily stroked Pat's shoulder. "Poor little kid. It's got to be better that he never knows his history."

"Speaking of history," said Sybil, stretching with a groan of luxury. "Noelle Winthall and Beth Chu are going to be very famous parents of cloned twins."

"After all the fuss, they're the only genuine clones the Halstead Clinic has produced," said Bourke.

Carol gave him a cynical smile. "That we know of," she said.

LOOKING FOR NAIAD?

Buy our books at
www.naiadpress.com

or call our toll-free number
1-800-533-1973

or by fax (24 hours a day)
1-850-539-9731

A few of the publications of
THE NAIAD PRESS, INC.
P.O. Box 10543   Tallahassee, Florida 32302
Phone (850) 539-5965
Toll-Free Order Number: 1-800-533-1973
Web Site: WWW.NAIADPRESS.COM
Mail orders welcome. Please include 15% postage.
Write or call for our free catalog which also features an
incredible selection of lesbian videos.

WINDROW GARDEN by Janet McClellan. 192 pp. They discover
a passion they never dreamed possible.   ISBN 1-56280-216-X $11.95

PAST DUE by Claire McNab. 224 pp. 10th Carol Ashton
mystery.   ISBN 1-56280-217-8   11.95

CHRISTABEL by Laura Adams. 224 pp. Two captive hearts and
the passion that will set them free.   ISBN 1-56280-214-3   11.95

PRIVATE PASSIONS by Laura DeHart Young. 192 pp. An
unforgettable new portrait of lesbian love . . .   ISBN 1-56280-215-1   11.95

BAD MOON RISING by Barbara Johnson. 208 pp. 2nd Colleen
Fitzgerald mystery.   ISBN 1-56280-211-9   11.95

RIVER QUAY by Janet McClellan. 208 pp. 3rd Tru North
mystery.   ISBN 1-56280-212-7   11.95

ENDLESS LOVE by Lisa Shapiro. 272 pp. To believe, once
again, that love can be forever.   ISBN 1-56280-213-5   11.95

FALLEN FROM GRACE by Pat Welch. 256 pp. 6th Helen Black
mystery.   ISBN 1-56280-209-7   11.95

THE NAKED EYE by Catherine Ennis. 208 pp. Her lover in the
camera's eye . . .   ISBN 1-56280-210-0   11.95

OVER THE LINE by Tracey Richardson. 176 pp. 2nd Stevie
Houston mystery.   ISBN 1-56280-202-X   11.95

JULIA'S SONG by Ann O'Leary. 208 pp. Strangely
disturbing . . . strangely exciting.   ISBN 1-56280-197-X   11.95

LOVE IN THE BALANCE by Marianne K. Martin. 256 pp.
Weighing the costs of love . . .   ISBN 1-56280-199-6   11.95

PIECE OF MY HEART by Julia Watts. 208 pp. All the
stuff that dreams are made of —   ISBN 1-56280-206-2   11.95

MAKING UP FOR LOST TIME by Karin Kallmaker. 240 pp.
Nobody does it better . . .   ISBN 1-56280-196-1   11.95

GOLD FEVER by Lyn Denison. 224 pp. By author of *Dream Lover.*   ISBN 1-56280-201-1   11.95

WHEN THE DEAD SPEAK by Therese Szymanski. 224 pp. 2nd Brett Higgins mystery.   ISBN 1-56280-198-8   11.95

FOURTH DOWN by Kate Calloway. 240 pp. 4th Cassidy James mystery.   ISBN 1-56280-205-4   11.95

A MOMENT'S INDISCRETION by Peggy J. Herring. 176 pp. There's a fine line between love and lust . . .   ISBN 1-56280-194-5   11.95

CITY LIGHTS/COUNTRY CANDLES by Penny Hayes. 208 pp. About the women she has known . . .   ISBN 1-56280-195-3   11.95

POSSESSIONS by Kaye Davis. 240 pp. 2nd Maris Middleton mystery.   ISBN 1-56280-192-9   11.95

A QUESTION OF LOVE by Saxon Bennett. 208 pp. Every woman is granted one great love.   ISBN 1-56280-205-4   11.95

RHYTHM TIDE by Frankie J. Jones. 160 pp. . . . to desire passionately and be passionately desired.   ISBN 1-56280-189-9   11.95

PENN VALLEY PHOENIX by Janet McClellan. 208 pp. 2nd Tru North Mystery.   ISBN 1-56280-200-3   11.95

BY RESERVATION ONLY by Jackie Calhoun. 240 pp. A chance for true happiness.   ISBN 1-56280-191-0   11.95

OLD BLACK MAGIC by Jaye Maiman. 272 pp. 9th Robin Miller mystery.   ISBN 1-56280-175-9   11.95

LEGACY OF LOVE by Marianne K. Martin. 240 pp. Women will do anything for her . . .   ISBN 1-56280-184-8   11.95

LETTING GO by Ann O'Leary. 160 pp. Laura, at 39, in love with 23-year-old Kate.   ISBN 1-56280-183-X   11.95

LADY BE GOOD edited by Barbara Grier and Christine Cassidy. 288 pp. Erotic stories by Naiad Press authors. ISBN 1-56280-180-5   14.95

CHAIN LETTER by Claire McNab. 288 pp. 9th Carol Ashton mystery.   ISBN 1-56280-181-3   11.95

NIGHT VISION by Laura Adams. 256 pp. Erotic fantasy romance by "famous" author.   ISBN 1-56280-182-1   11.95

SEA TO SHINING SEA by Lisa Shapiro. 256 pp. Unable to resist the raging passion . . .   ISBN 1-56280-177-5   11.95

THIRD DEGREE by Kate Calloway. 224 pp. 3rd Cassidy James mystery.   ISBN 1-56280-185-6   11.95

WHEN THE DANCING STOPS by Therese Szymanski. 272 pp. 1st Brett Higgins mystery.   ISBN 1-56280-186-4   11.95

PHASES OF THE MOON by Julia Watts. 192 pp. . . . . . hungry for everything life has to offer.   ISBN 1-56280-176-7   11.95

BABY IT'S COLD by Jaye Maiman. 256 pp. 5th Robin Miller mystery.   ISBN 1-56280-156-2   10.95

SMOKE AND MIRRORS by Pat Welch. 224 pp. 5th Helen Black
Mystery.   ISBN 1-56280-143-0   10.95

DANCING IN THE DARK edited by Barbara Grier & Christine
Cassidy. 272 pp. Erotic love stories by Naiad Press authors.
                                                ISBN 1-56280-144-9   14.95

TIME AND TIME AGAIN by Catherine Ennis. 176 pp. Passionate
love affair.   ISBN 1-56280-145-7   10.95

PAXTON COURT by Diane Salvatore. 256 pp. Erotic and wickedly
funny contemporary tale about the business of learning to live
together.   ISBN 1-56280-114-7   10.95

INNER CIRCLE by Claire McNab. 208 pp. 8th Carol Ashton
Mystery.   ISBN 1-56280-135-X   11.95

LESBIAN SEX: AN ORAL HISTORY by Susan Johnson.
240 pp. Need we say more?   ISBN 1-56280-142-2   14.95

WILD THINGS by Karin Kallmaker. 240 pp. By the undisputed
mistress of lesbian romance.   ISBN 1-56280-139-2   11.95

THE GIRL NEXT DOOR by Mindy Kaplan. 208 pp. Just what
you d expect.   ISBN 1-56280-140-6   11.95

NOW AND THEN by Penny Hayes. 240 pp. Romance on the
westward journey.   ISBN 1-56280-121-X   11.95

HEART ON FIRE by Diana Simmonds. 176 pp. The romantic and
erotic rival of *Curious Wine*.   ISBN 1-56280-152-X   11.95

DEATH AT LAVENDER BAY by Lauren Wright Douglas. 208 pp.
1st Allison O'Neil Mystery.   ISBN 1-56280-085-X   11.95

YES I SAID YES I WILL by Judith McDaniel. 272 pp. Hot
romance by famous author.   ISBN 1-56280-138-4   11.95

FORBIDDEN FIRES by Margaret C. Anderson. Edited by Mathilda
Hills. 176 pp. Famous author's "unpublished" Lesbian romance.
                                                ISBN 1-56280-123-6   21.95

SIDE TRACKS by Teresa Stores. 160 pp. Gender-bending
Lesbians on the road.   ISBN 1-56280-122-8   10.95

HOODED MURDER by Annette Van Dyke. 176 pp. 1st Jessie
Batelle Mystery.   ISBN 1-56280-134-1   10.95

WILDWOOD FLOWERS by Julia Watts. 208 pp. Hilarious and
heart-warming tale of true love.   ISBN 1-56280-127-9   10.95

NEVER SAY NEVER by Linda Hill. 224 pp. Rule #1: Never get
involved with . . .   ISBN 1-56280-126-0   11.95

THE SEARCH by Melanie McAllester. 240 pp. Exciting top cop
Tenny Mendoza case.   ISBN 1-56280-150-3   10.95

THE WISH LIST by Saxon Bennett. 192 pp. Romance through
the years.   ISBN 1-56280-125-2   10.95

FIRST IMPRESSIONS by Kate 208 pp. 1st P.I. Cassidy
James mystery.   ISBN 1-56280-133-3   10.95

OUT OF THE NIGHT by Kris Bruyer. 192 pp. Spine-tingling
thriller.   ISBN 1-56280-120-1   10.95

NORTHERN BLUE by Tracey Richardson. 224 pp. Police recruits
Miki & Miranda — passion in the line of fire. ISBN 1-56280-118-X   10.95

LOVE'S HARVEST by Peggy J. Herring. 176 pp. by the author of
Once More With Feeling.   ISBN 1-56280-117-1   10.95

THE COLOR OF WINTER by Lisa Shapiro. 208 pp. Romantic
love beyond your wildest dreams.   ISBN 1-56280-116-3   10.95

FAMILY SECRETS by Laura DeHart Young. 208 pp. Enthralling
romance and suspense.   ISBN 1-56280-119-8   10.95

INLAND PASSAGE by Jane Rule. 288 pp. Tales exploring conventional & unconventional relationships.   ISBN 0-930044-56-8   10.95

DOUBLE BLUFF by Claire McNab. 208 pp. 7th Carol Ashton
Mystery.   ISBN 1-56280-096-5   10.95

BAR GIRLS by Lauran Hoffman. 176 pp. See the movie, read
the book!   ISBN 1-56280-115-5   10.95

THE FIRST TIME EVER edited by Barbara Grier & Christine
Cassidy. 272 pp. Love stories by Naiad Press authors.
                                            ISBN 1-56280-086-8   14.95

MISS PETTIBONE AND MISS McGRAW by Brenda Weathers.
208 pp. A charming ghostly love story.   ISBN 1-56280-151-1   10.95

CHANGES by Jackie Calhoun. 208 pp. Involved romance and
relationships.   ISBN 1-56280-083-3   10.95

FAIR PLAY by Rose Beecham. 256 pp. An Amanda Valentine
Mystery.   ISBN 1-56280-081-7   10.95

PAYBACK by Celia Cohen. 176 pp. A gripping thriller of romance,
revenge and betrayal.   ISBN 1-56280-084-1   10.95

THE BEACH AFFAIR by Barbara Johnson. 224 pp. Sizzling
summer romance/mystery/intrigue.   ISBN 1-56280-090-6   10.95

GETTING THERE by Robbi Sommers. 192 pp. Nobody does it
like Robbi!   ISBN 1-56280-099-X   10.95

FINAL CUT by Lisa Haddock. 208 pp. 2nd Carmen Ramirez
Mystery.   ISBN 1-56280-088-4   10.95

FLASHPOINT by Katherine V. Forrest. 256 pp. A Lesbian
blockbuster!   ISBN 1-56280-079-5   10.95

CLAIRE OF THE MOON by Nicole Conn. Audio Book —
Read by Marianne Hyatt.   ISBN 1-56280-113-9   16.95

FOR LOVE AND FOR LIFE: INTIMATE PORTRAITS OF
LESBIAN COUPLES by Susan Johnson. 224 pp.
                                            ISBN 1-56280-091-4   14.95

DEVOTION by Mindy Kaplan. 192 pp. See the movie — read the book! ISBN 1-56280-093-0 10.95

SOMEONE TO WATCH by Jaye Maiman. 272 pp. 4th Robin Miller Mystery. ISBN 1-56280-095-7 10.95

GREENER THAN GRASS by Jennifer Fulton. 208 pp. A young woman — a stranger in her bed. ISBN 1-56280-092-2 10.95

TRAVELS WITH DIANA HUNTER by Regine Sands. Erotic lesbian romp. Audio Book (2 cassettes) ISBN 1-56280-107-4 16.95

CABIN FEVER by Carol Schmidt. 256 pp. Sizzling suspense and passion. ISBN 1-56280-089-1 10.95

THERE WILL BE NO GOODBYES by Laura DeHart Young. 192 pp. Romantic love, strength, and friendship. ISBN 1-56280-103-1 10.95

FAULTLINE by Sheila Ortiz Taylor. 144 pp. Joyous comic lesbian novel. ISBN 1-56280-108-2 9.95

OPEN HOUSE by Pat Welch. 176 pp. 4th Helen Black Mystery. ISBN 1-56280-102-3 10.95

ONCE MORE WITH FEELING by Peggy J. Herring. 240 pp. Lighthearted, loving romantic adventure. ISBN 1-56280-089-2 11.95

FOREVER by Evelyn Kennedy. 224 pp. Passionate romance — love overcoming all obstacles. ISBN 1-56280-094-9 10.95

WHISPERS by Kris Bruyer. 176 pp. Romantic ghost story. ISBN 1-56280-082-5 10.95

NIGHT SONGS by Penny Mickelbury. 224 pp. 2nd Gianna Maglione Mystery. ISBN 1-56280-097-3 10.95

GETTING TO THE POINT by Teresa Stores. 256 pp. Classic southern Lesbian novel. ISBN 1-56280-100-7 10.95

PAINTED MOON by Karin Kallmaker. 224 pp. Delicious Kallmaker romance. ISBN 1-56280-075-2 11.95

THE MYSTERIOUS NAIAD edited by Katherine V. Forrest & Barbara Grier. 320 pp. Love stories by Naiad Press authors. ISBN 1-56280-074-4 14.95

DAUGHTERS OF A CORAL DAWN by Katherine V. Forrest. 240 pp. Tenth Anniversay Edition. ISBN 1-56280-104-X 11.95

BODY GUARD by Claire McNab. 208 pp. 6th Carol Ashton Mystery. ISBN 1-56280-073-6 11.95

CACTUS LOVE by Lee Lynch. 192 pp. Stories by the beloved storyteller. ISBN 1-56280-071-X 9.95

SECOND GUESS by Rose Beecham. 216 pp. An Amanda Valentine Mystery. ISBN 1-56280-069-8 9.95

A RAGE OF MAIDENS by Lauren Wright Douglas. 240 pp. 6th Caitlin Reece Mystery. ISBN 1-56280-068-X 10.95

TRIPLE EXPOSURE by Jackie Calhoun. 224 pp. Romantic
drama involving many characters.   ISBN 1-56280-067-1   10.95

PERSONAL ADS by Robbi Sommers. 176 pp. Sizzling short
stories.   ISBN 1-56280-059-0   11.95

CROSSWORDS by Penny Sumner. 256 pp. 2nd Victoria Cross
Mystery.   ISBN 1-56280-064-7   9.95

SWEET CHERRY WINE by Carol Schmidt. 224 pp. A novel of
suspense.   ISBN 1-56280-063-9   9.95

CERTAIN SMILES by Dorothy Tell. 160 pp. Erotic short stories.
ISBN 1-56280-066-3   9.95

EDITED OUT by Lisa Haddock. 224 pp. 1st Carmen Ramirez
Mystery.   ISBN 1-56280-077-9   9.95

WEDNESDAY NIGHTS by Camarin Grae. 288 pp. Sexy
adventure.   ISBN 1-56280-060-4   11.95

SMOKEY O by Celia Cohen. 176 pp. Relationships on the
playing field.   ISBN 1-56280-057-4   9.95

KATHLEEN O'DONALD by Penny Hayes. 256 pp. Rose and
Kathleen find each other and employment in 1909 NYC.
ISBN 1-56280-070-1   9.95

STAYING HOME by Elisabeth Nonas. 256 pp. Molly and Alix
want a baby . . . or do they?   ISBN 1-56280-076-0   10.95

TRUE LOVE by Jennifer Fulton. 240 pp. Six lesbians searching
for love in all the "right" places.   ISBN 1-56280-035-3   11.95

KEEPING SECRETS by Penny Mickelbury. 208 pp. 1st Gianna
Maglione Mystery.   ISBN 1-56280-052-3   9.95

THE ROMANTIC NAIAD edited by Katherine V. Forrest &
Barbara Grier. 336 pp. Love stories by Naiad Press authors.
ISBN 1-56280-054-X   14.95

UNDER MY SKIN by Jaye Maiman. 336 pp. 3rd Robin Miller
Mystery.   ISBN 1-56280-049-3.   11.95

CAR POOL by Karin Kallmaker. 272pp. Lesbians on wheels
and then some!   ISBN 1-56280-048-5   11.95

NOT TELLING MOTHER: STORIES FROM A LIFE by Diane
Salvatore. 176 pp. Her 3rd novel.   ISBN 1-56280-044-2   9.95

GOBLIN MARKET by Lauren Wright Douglas. 240pp. 5th Caitlin
Reece Mystery.   ISBN 1-56280-047-7   10.95

FRIENDS AND LOVERS by Jackie Calhoun. 224 pp. Mid-
western Lesbian lives and loves.   ISBN 1-56280-041-8   11.95

BEHIND CLOSED DOORS by Robbi Sommers. 192 pp. Hot,
erotic short stories.   ISBN 1-56280-039-6   11.95

CLAIRE OF THE MOON by Nicole Conn. 192 pp. See the
movie — read the book!   ISBN 1-56280-038-8   11.95

SILENT HEART by Claire McNab. 192 pp. Exotic Lesbian
romance.   ISBN 1-56280-036-1   11.95

THE SPY IN QUESTION by Amanda Kyle Williams. 256 pp.
A Madison McGuire Mystery.   ISBN 1-56280-037-X   9.95

SAVING GRACE by Jennifer Fulton. 240 pp. Adventure and
romantic entanglement.   ISBN 1-56280-051-5   11.95

CURIOUS WINE by Katherine V. Forrest. 176 pp. Tenth Anniver-
sary Edition. The most popular contemporary Lesbian love story.
                                             ISBN 1-56280-053-1   11.95
        Audio Book (2 cassettes)   ISBN 1-56280-105-8   16.95

CHAUTAUQUA by Catherine Ennis. 192 pp. Exciting, romantic
adventure.   ISBN 1-56280-032-9   9.95

A PROPER BURIAL by Pat Welch. 192 pp. 3rd Helen Black
Mystery.   ISBN 1-56280-033-7   9.95

SILVERLAKE HEAT: A Novel of Suspense by Carol Schmidt.
240 pp. Rhonda is as hot as Laney's dreams. ISBN 1-56280-031-0   9.95

LOVE, ZENA BETH by Diane Salvatore. 224 pp. The most talked
about lesbian novel of the nineties!   ISBN 1-56280-030-2   10.95

A DOORYARD FULL OF FLOWERS by Isabel Miller. 160 pp.
Stories incl. 2 sequels to *Patience and Sarah.* ISBN 1-56280-029-9 9.95

MURDER BY TRADITION by Katherine V. Forrest. 288 pp. 4th
Kate Delafield Mystery.   ISBN 1-56280-002-7   11.95

THE EROTIC NAIAD edited by Katherine V. Forrest & Barbara
Grier. 224 pp. Love stories by Naiad Press authors.
                                             ISBN 1-56280-026-4   14.95

DEAD CERTAIN by Claire McNab. 224 pp. 5th Carol Ashton
Mystery.   ISBN 1-56280-027-2   9.95

CRAZY FOR LOVING by Jaye Maiman. 320 pp. 2nd Robin Miller
Mystery.   ISBN 1-56280-025-6   11.95

UNCERTAIN COMPANIONS by Robbi Sommers. 204 pp.
Steamy, erotic novel.   ISBN 1-56280-017-5   11.95

A TIGER'S HEART by Lauren W. Douglas. 240 pp. 4th Caitlin
Reece Mystery.   ISBN 1-56280-018-3   9.95

PAPERBACK ROMANCE by Karin Kallmaker. 256 pp. A
delicious romance.   ISBN 1-56280-019-1   10.95

THE LAVENDER HOUSE MURDER by Nikki Baker. 224 pp.
2nd Virginia Kelly Mystery.   ISBN 1-56280-012-4   9.95

PASSION BAY by Jennifer Fulton. 224 pp. Passionate romance,
virgin beaches, tropical skies.   ISBN 1-56280-028-0   10.95

STICKS AND STONES by Jackie Calhoun. 208 pp. Contemporary
lesbian lives and loves.   ISBN 1-56280-020-5   9.95
Audio Book (2 cassettes)   ISBN 1-56280-106-6   16.95

UNDER THE SOUTHERN CROSS by Claire McNab. 192 pp.
Romantic nights Down Under.   ISBN 1-56280-011-6   11.95

GRASSY FLATS by Penny Hayes. 256 pp. Lesbian romance in
the '30s.   ISBN 1-56280-010-8   9.95

THE END OF APRIL by Penny Sumner. 240 pp. 1st Victoria
Cross Mystery.   ISBN 1-56280-007-8   8.95

KISS AND TELL by Robbi Sommers. 192 pp. Scorching stories
by the author of *Pleasures*.   ISBN 1-56280-005-1   11.95

STILL WATERS by Pat Welch. 208 pp. 2nd Helen Black Mystery.
                                           ISBN 0-941483-97-5   9.95

TO LOVE AGAIN by Evelyn Kennedy. 208 pp. Wildly romantic
love story.   ISBN 0-941483-85-1   11.95

IN THE GAME by Nikki Baker. 192 pp. 1st Virginia Kelly
Mystery.   ISBN 1-56280-004-3   9.95

STRANDED by Camarin Grae. 320 pp. Entertaining, riveting
adventure.   ISBN 0-941483-99-1   9.95

THE DAUGHTERS OF ARTEMIS by Lauren Wright Douglas.
240 pp. 3rd Caitlin Reece Mystery.   ISBN 0-941483-95-9   9.95

CLEARWATER by Catherine Ennis. 176 pp. Romantic secrets
of a small Louisiana town.   ISBN 0-941483-65-7   8.95

THE HALLELUJAH MURDERS by Dorothy Tell. 176 pp. 2nd
Poppy Dillworth Mystery.   ISBN 0-941483-88-6   8.95

SECOND CHANCE by Jackie Calhoun. 256 pp. Contemporary
Lesbian lives and loves.   ISBN 0-941483-93-2   9.95

BENEDICTION by Diane Salvatore. 272 pp. Striking, contemporary romantic novel.   ISBN 0-941483-90-8   11.95

TOUCHWOOD by Karin Kallmaker. 240 pp. Loving, May/
December romance.   ISBN 0-941483-76-2   11.95

COP OUT by Claire McNab. 208 pp. 4th Carol Ashton Mystery.
                                           ISBN 0-941483-84-3   10.95

THE BEVERLY MALIBU by Katherine V. Forrest. 288 pp. 3rd
Kate Delafield Mystery.   ISBN 0-941483-48-7   11.95

THE PROVIDENCE FILE by Amanda Kyle Williams. 256 pp.
A Madison McGuire Mystery.   ISBN 0-941483-92-4   8.95

I LEFT MY HEART by Jaye Maiman. 320 pp. 1st Robin Miller
Mystery.   ISBN 0-941483-72-X   11.95

THE PRICE OF SALT by Patricia Highsmith (writing as Claire
Morgan). 288 pp. Classic lesbian novel, first issued in 1952 . . .
acknowledged by its author under her own, very famous, name.
                                           ISBN 1-56280-003-5   11.95

SIDE BY SIDE by Isabel Miller. 256 pp. From beloved author of
Patience and Sarah.   ISBN 0-941483-77-0   10.95

STAYING POWER: LONG TERM LESBIAN COUPLES by
Susan E. Johnson. 352 pp. Joys of coupledom. ISBN 0-941-483-75-4   14.95

SLICK by Camarin Grae. 304 pp. Exotic, erotic adventure.
ISBN 0-941483-74-6   9.95

NINTH LIFE by Lauren Wright Douglas. 256 pp. 2nd Caitlin
Reece Mystery.   ISBN 0-941483-50-9   9.95

PLAYERS by Robbi Sommers. 192 pp. Sizzling, erotic novel.
ISBN 0-941483-73-8   9.95

MURDER AT RED ROOK RANCH by Dorothy Tell. 224 pp.
1st Poppy Dillworth Mystery.   ISBN 0-941483-80-0   8.95

A ROOM FULL OF WOMEN by Elisabeth Nonas. 256 pp.
Contemporary Lesbian lives.   ISBN 0-941483-69-X   9.95

THEME FOR DIVERSE INSTRUMENTS by Jane Rule. 208 pp.
Powerful romantic lesbian stories.   ISBN 0-941483-63-0   8.95

CLUB 12 by Amanda Kyle Williams. 288 pp. Espionage thriller
featuring a lesbian agent!   ISBN 0-941483-64-9   9.95

DEATH DOWN UNDER by Claire McNab. 240 pp. 3rd Carol
Ashton Mystery.   ISBN 0-941483-39-8   10.95

MONTANA FEATHERS by Penny Hayes. 256 pp. Vivian and
Elizabeth find love in frontier Montana.   ISBN 0-941483-61-4   9.95

LIFESTYLES by Jackie Calhoun. 224 pp. Contemporary Lesbian
lives and loves.   ISBN 0-941483-57-6   10.95

MURDER BY THE BOOK by Pat Welch. 256 pp. 1st Helen
Black Mystery.   ISBN 0-941483-59-2   9.95

THERE'S SOMETHING I'VE BEEN MEANING TO TELL YOU
Ed. by Loralee MacPike. 288 pp. Gay men and lesbians coming out
to their children.   ISBN 0-941483-44-4   9.95

LIFTING BELLY by Gertrude Stein. Ed. by Rebecca Mark. 104 pp.
Erotic poetry.   ISBN 0-941483-51-7   10.95

AFTER THE FIRE by Jane Rule. 256 pp. Warm, human novel by
this incomparable author.   ISBN 0-941483-45-2   8.95

PLEASURES by Robbi Sommers. 204 pp. Unprecedented
eroticism.   ISBN 0-941483-49-5   11.95

EDGEWISE by Camarin Grae. 372 pp. Spellbinding
adventure.   ISBN 0-941483-19-3   9.95

These are just a few of the many Naiad Press titles — we are the oldest and
largest lesbian/feminist publishing company in the world. We also offer an
enormous selection of lesbian video products. Please request a complete
catalog. We offer personal service; we encourage and welcome direct mail
orders from individuals who have limited access to bookstores carrying our
publications.